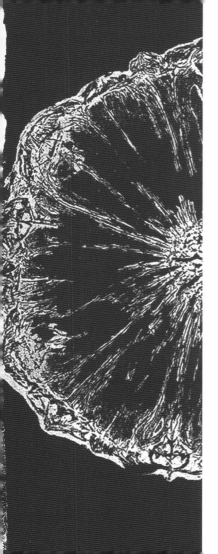

imagine africa

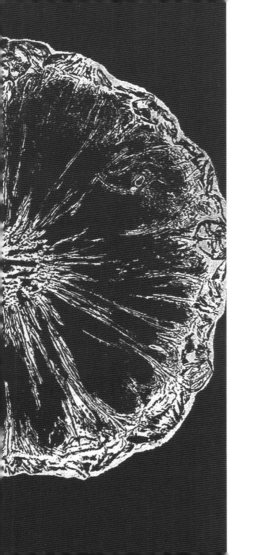

imagine africa

Pirogue

ISLAND POSITION

Brooklyn · Cape Town · Gorée · Paris

2016

Island Position is grateful for the generous support of the Eva Tas Foundation.

"Heart of Darkness" by Chika Unigwe, copyright © Chika Unigwe.
Originally appeared at Citybooks.
Used by permission of Wolf Literary Servives, LLC. All rights reserved.

Excerpt from *La Divine Chanson* © Abdourahman Waberi, 2015.

Excerpt from *Photo de groupe au bord du fleuve* by permission from the author Emmanuel Dongala.

COVER ART

Hassan Hajjaj, *Ilham*, 2000, digital C-print, 94 x 129 cm,
courtesy the artist and Taymour Grahne Gallery, New York.

PHOTOGRAPHY AND ART CREDITS

Page 22: Hassan Hajjaj, *Poetic Pilgrimage*, 2010, metallic lambda print on 3mm dibond, 136 x 100.6 cm.
Page 86: Hassan Hajjaj, *Wamuhu*, 2015.
Page 114: Hassan Hajjaj, *Kesh Angels*, 2010, metallic lambda print on 3mm dibond, 101 x 137.7cm.
Page 142: Hassan Hajjaj, *Hindiii*, 2011, metallic lambda print on 3mm disband, 120 x 85 cm.
All images courtesy the artist and Taymour Grahne Gallery, New York.

Page 33: Zanele Muholi, *Massa and Minah I*, 2008. • Page 34: Zanele Muholi, *Massa and Minah VI*, 2010.
Page 35: Zanele Muholi, *Massa and Maids IV*, Hout Bay, 2009. • Page 36: Zanele Muholi, *Massa and Minah II,* 2008.
Page 37: Zanele Muholi, *Massa and Minah III*, 2008. • Page 38: Zanele Muholi, *Minah V*, 2009.
All images courtesy of Stevenson, Cape Town and Johannesburg.

Page 144: Jean-Pierre Bekolo, *An African Woman in Space*, Musée du Quai Branly Paris, 2007–8.
Pages 148–149: Jean-Pierre Bekolo scene from Le président, 2013.
Page 156: Jean-Pierre Bekolo, scene from *An African Woman in Space*, Musée du Quai Branly Paris, 2007–8.
All images courtesy of Jean-Pierre Bekolo.

PRINTED BY THOMSON-SHORE IN THE UNITED STATES

Contents

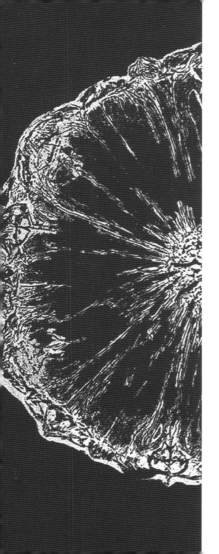

imagine africa

ABDOURAHMAN WABERI
Translated from the French by DAVID and NICOLE BALL

La Divine Chanson
un extrait

The Divine Song
an excerpt

LILY WILLIAMS, la grand-mère de Sammy, avait eu la chance de connaître son arrière-arrière-grand-mère née en Afrique. C'était une très belle femme. Grande de taille, le teint couleur nuit. Elle avait vu le jour dans la cour d'un grand roi. Aux enfants, l'ancêtre rapportait que tous les Noirs achetés par les Blancs ne devenaient pas esclaves. À l'époque, dans cette cour royale, éclairée par six torches baignant dans la résine d'okoumé, le sel était un produit précieux et son grand-père était chargé de l'éclairage. Elle racontait que la vie était agréable

LILY WILLIAMS, Sammy's grandmother, was lucky enough to have known his great-great-grandmother, who was born in Africa. She was a very beautiful woman. Tall, with her skin the color of night. She came into the world in the court of a great king. The old woman told the children that all the Blacks bought by the Whites did not become slaves. At the time, in this royal court, lit by six torches dipped in okoumé resin, salt was a precious product; her grandfather was in charge of lighting. She said that life was pleasant before the arrival of the soul-eaters. But

Djiboutian novelist, essayist, academic, and poet **ABDOURAHMAN WABERI** arrived in France in 1985 to study English literature. While in Paris, Waberi was a literary consultant for Editions Le Serpent à plumes and a literary critic for *Le Monde Diplomatique*. Waberi's first collection of stories *Le Pays Sans Ombre* (1994) received the Grand prix de la nouvelle francophone from the Académie Royale de Langue et de Littérature Française de Belgique and the Prix Albert Bernard from the Académie des Sciences d'Outre-mer de Paris. A versatile writer, he is the author of almost a dozen books and has been translated into over ten languages. He currently teaches at George Washington University.

avant l'arrivée des mangeurs d'âmes.
Mais la joie s'est éteinte peu à peu. Dès
la tombée de la nuit, les villages étaient
déserts. Les mangeurs d'âmes rôdaient,
précédés par les hyènes, les chacals et
les vautours. Tous les Noirs ne deve-
naient pas esclaves, répétait la vieille
pour nos oreilles innocentes. Il arrivait
souvent que des captifs disparais-
sent au cours du voyage, échappant
définitivement à l'esclavage. Volatilisés.
Ils avaient des méthodes particulières
et des fétiches qui leur assuraient
l'accès à l'inconnu en empruntant des
chemins escarpés et dangereux.

Grandir auprès de mes parents
d'Afrique fut une chance inouïe,
soufflait-elle, car j'eus tôt l'occasion
d'écouter de nombreuses histoires.
En ce temps-la, racontait l'ancêtre
baptisée Adelina, pour être une bonne
personne il fallait se doter, à la prime
adolescence, de pouvoirs surnat-
urels. Les grands-parents avaient la
charge de voir grandir leurs petits-
enfants avant de leur transmettre les

little by little, all joy was extinguished.
As soon as night fell, the villages were
deserted. The soul-eaters would go out
on the prowl, preceded by hyenas, jack-
als and vultures.

All the Blacks did not become
slaves, the old woman repeated for
our innocent ears. Often captives
would disappear during the voyage,
definitively escaping from slavery.
Vanished into thin air. They had spe-
cial ways and fetishes that assured
their access to the unknown by tak-
ing steep, dangerous paths.

Growing up with my African parents
was an incredible piece of luck, she
would whisper, for from an early age, I
had the opportunity to listen to many
stories. In those days, said the old lady
named Adelina, to be a good person
you had to acquire supernatural powers
in yout early adolescence. It was the
duty of the grandparents to see their
grandchildren reach adolescence before
they could transmit to them the secrets
surrounding the preparation of magic

secrets entourant la préparation des breuvages. La confection des fétiches et des reliques se pratiquait, à l'écart du monde visible, au fond de la forêt. Et les Noirs de la côte, alliés des Blancs, étaient très intéressés par les pouvoirs surnaturels. Alléchés. Attirés par l'odeur du sang, ils se lançaient a la recherche des fétiches, sillonnant les terres profondes, tuant tout sur leur passage. Mais les hommes de la forêt savaient manier le coutelas. Rien ne pouvait leur résister, pas même l'assaut des troupeaux de buffles. Si d'aventure, ils étaient pris par les courtiers de la côte, ligotés, destinés à être livrés aux Blancs, il suffisait aux hommes de la forêt d'un mot de passe pour que les liens se brisent sans délai. Ils s'enfuyaient. Une fois, deux fois, dix fois. Mais malheureusement pour eux, les hommes de la forêt n'allaient pas tous tres loin parce que les Blancs les tuaient avec leurs longs fusils. D'autres, pris de panique, se disaient : «Il faut rester calme parce

potions. Making fetishes and relics was practiced away from the visible world, in the depths of the forest. And the Blacks of the Coast who were the Whites' allies were extremely interested in supernatural powers. It made their mouth water. Attracted by the smell of blood, they threw themselves into the search for fetishes, walking back and forth over the deepest reaches of the land, killing everything in their path. But the men of the forest were adept at using the cutlass. Nothing could resist them, not even an assault by a herd of water-buffalo. If by chance they were captured by the courtiers of the coast, tied up and ready to be delivered to the Whites, all the men of the forest needed was a password for their bonds to be sundered immediately. They fled. Once, twice, ten times. But unfortunately for them, the men of the forest could not all get very far because the Whites would kill them with their long rifles. Others would panic and say to themselves: "We must stay calm because the

DAVID and NICOLE BALL have signed, together or separately, well over a dozen book-length translations, including three novels by Abdourahman A. Waberi, and most recently *Marseille Noir* for Akashic Books. They are currently working on *The Divine Song* for Seagull Books. David won the French-American Foundation 2014 Translation Prize (non-fiction) for *Jean Guéhenno, Diary of the Dark Years: 1940-1944* (Oxford University Press) and MLA's prize for outstanding literary translation in 1995 for *Darkness Moves: An Henri Michaux Anthology 1927-1984* (University of California Press.) His translation of Alfred Jarry's *Ubu the King* is included in the Norton Anthology of Drama. Nicole has translated three books from French to English, among them Maryse Condé's *Land of Many Colors* (University of Nebraska Press.)

que le bâton que tient le Blanc peut tuer un éléphant.» C'est ainsi, disait la grand-mère de ma grand-mère baptisée Adelina en hommage à une religieuse espagnole, qu'on embarquait les hommes de la forêt défaits par les fétiches des Blancs.

Les fuyards s'enfonçaient dans la forêt, se terrant dans les massifs de Mbelet et de Mamfoumbi, quêtant de nouveaux fétiches. Les résultats ne furent pas toujours à la hauteur. La grand-mère de ma grand-mère Adelina avait entendu dire que les pouvoirs de certains féticheurs ne se réveillaient que les nuits sans lune. Les Blancs entendaient, de loin, les grognements de la panthère qui protégeait la cour d'Ouidah et au même moment, la carcasse d'un esclave s'agitait au fond de la cale. Pris de peur, les Blancs se disaient : «Regarde-le! Ses yeux sortent de l'orbite. Il a les poils de la panthère. Que faire? Il est en transe.» Sans plus attendre, les Blancs le jetaient

stick in the hands of the White man can kill an elephant." This, said my grandmother's grandmother, named Adelina in honor of a Spanish nun, is how they carried off the men of the forest, defeated by the fetishes of the Whites.

The ones who fled would plunge deep into the forest, hiding in the Mbelet and Mamfumbi mountains, searching for new fetishes. The results did not always measure up. My grandmother Adelina's grandmother had heard that the powers of some fetish-makers would only awake on moonless nights. The Whites would hear the far-off growls of the panther that protected the Ouidah court and at the exact same time, the carcass of a slave would begin to jerk around at the bottom of the hold. Frightened, the Whites said to themselves: "Look at him! His eyes are coming out of their sockets. He has the hair of a panther. What can we do? He's in a trance." Without delay, the Whites would throw him overboard. On

donc par-dessus bord. Au contact de l'eau, les esprits libéraient l'écrin charnel et s'en allaient. Et l'esclave ou, plus exactement, son enveloppe mourait par noyade au large. Tandis que sa part éthérée, sempiternellement neuve, retournait dans la forêt comme ça, sur un claquement de doigts. Voilà ce que me racontait la grand-mère de ma grand-mère baptisée Adelina en hommage à une religieuse catholique qui venait en aide aux Noirs de la Floride. Et voilà ce que je racontais moi-même à mon petit Sammy baptisé en l'honneur d'un ancêtre au masque pommelé de taches de rousseur comme s'il était sorti d'un brasier. Cet ancêtre nègre rouquin avait connu la religieuse espagnole. Il s'appelait Samuel lui aussi.

Lily n'était pas une femme ordinaire. Elle avait l'art du conteur chevillé au corps. Et comme le diseur des sept vérités, elle déroulait ses récits ésotériques tout en gardant pour elle leurs codes et leurs énigmes. L'histoire finie,

contact with the water, the spirits would free his fleshly envelope and leave. And the slave, or, more exactly, his mortal coil, would die of drowning out at sea. While his ethereal part, eternally renewed, would return to the forest just like that, at the snap of a finger. That is what was told to me by the grandmother of my grandmother named Adelina in honor of a Spanish nun who came to the assistance of the Blacks of Florida. And that's what I myself told my little Sammy, baptized Sammy in honor of an ancestor whose face was all spotted with red freckles as if he had come out of an inferno. This black redheaded ancestor had known the Spanish nun. His name was Samuel, too.

Lilly was not an ordinary woman. She was a born storyteller. And like the teller of the seven truths, she would roll out her esoteric stories while keeping their codes and enigmas to herself. Once the story was over, she would pick up her bundle

The original French edition of *La Divine Chanson* has a red paper band across the cover with, in English, "The revolution will not be televised" on it. This lyrical novel is a fictionalized life of that internationally known spoken-word song's author—Gil Scott-Heron, here called Sammy Kamau-Williams. His story is told by Paris, his magical Sufi cat, with special emphasis on Scott-Heron's roots in the Caribbean and Africa, and his links to Brazil.

elle reprenait son baluchon, elle se levait d'un bond pour retourner à ses grandes bassines en inox. À ses draps et le reste de son linge à laver car elle nourrit ses enfants et ses petits-enfants à la force de ses poignets couverts de mousse de savon. Il ne restait plus qu'à guetter la prochaine occasion. Les soirs d'été, les fêtes spontanées ne manquaient pas. Le parc et l'arrière-cour de l'église étaient pleins comme un œuf. Mariages, baptêmes, récoltes, arrivées de nouveaux dans le voisinage, toutes les occasions étaient bonnes. Les membres de la famille, les voisins, les métayers des bourgs environnants, les chanteurs ambulants, les ouailles de la paroisse et les pèlerins d'un soir se retrouvaient pour d'interminables victuailles suivies d'interminables danses et célébrations.

Les récits de l'ancêtre agissaient comme un révélateur. Toute la lignée en gardait la trace, à son insu. Lily fut de ceux qui tiraient la famille vers la lumière, la clarté du jour, les aubes au détriment des crépuscules.

again, spring to her feet and return to her big stainless steel basins. To her sheets and the rest of the wash, for she fed her children and grandchildren by means of her soapsud-cover wrists. All one could do was wait for the next occasion. On summer evenings, there was no lack of spontaneous festivities. The grounds and backyard of the church were full to bursting. Weddings, baptisms, harvests, the arrival of new people in the neighborhood, any occasion was matter for celebration. Members of the family, neighbors, tenant farmers of surrounding towns, wandering singers, the parishioners and the passing pilgrims would all come together for interminable feasts followed by interminable dances and celebrations.

The old woman's stories were a revelation. Her whole lineage kept a trace of them without knowing it. Lilly was one of those people who could draw a family toward the light, the light of day, to dawns and never to sunsets.

REESOM HAILE

Translated from the Tigrinya by CHARLES CANTALUPO

Habereita nWashington

entay qeribkley abti eton
nA zbelkni Washington

eta buney
aSelm ablya

eta engeiray
aSaEduw ablya

eta SebHey
aQiH ablya

qeTelya meTelya keytblni
qeTelya meTelya nTeil,ya

entay qeribkley abti eton
nA zbelkni Washington

My Washington Agenda

You want to invite me?
What's in the oven?
Mmmmm…eat!

I like my coffee black,
My bread white,
And my sauce red,

But your greens,
Please, give them
To the goats.
You know what I mean?

You want to invite me?
What's in the oven?
Mmmmeat!

REESOM HAILE, 1946–2003, remains Eritrea's most famous contemporary poet. In exile during Eritrea's war for independence, he returned there in 1994. His first and only collection in Tigrinya, *Waza Ms Qumneger Ntnsae Hager* ("Your Knowing Smiles"), won the 1998 Raimok prize, Eritrea's highest award for literature. He patriotically rallied his nation with a poem that achieved the popularity of a rock 'n' roll anthem, "Alewuna, Alewana," "We Have, We Have." Celebrating independence from European colonialism, many an African nation would echo and translate William Wordsworth's famous words: "Bliss was it in that dawn to be alive / But to be young was very heaven." As the 1990s unfolded, Eritrea embodied it loud and clear. Living in Asmara, Eritrea's capital, Haile was constantly high-spirited. His poems consistently exhibited a playful tone or, in his more serious lyrics, a playful edge. They also provided a window to see Eritrea as it had never been seen before and, perhaps, has never been seen since.

mereret /qWereret

adam wedi Qedam
tefeTre / af aTre

wSíe ilu kurba
jemere medere

Alem teberaberi
ente día ktnebri
kab SbaH senuy
zbelkuwo tgebri

etlgselu Tafa
keytmlselu beyanay afa

zdeleyo neygeberet
mereret día qWereret

Bitter and Cold

Born on the sixth day,
Adam
Has the power
To say

"Hey, World.
You better listen to me.
Obey,
If you want to live."

But she
Has the power
To give
Or take away.

emo barnet aleka!

wedi Qedam
kem enssa zebeitdo
kem enssa zegedam?

kníedo do kewardo?

eske awardo!

adgi! beQli! bEray!

eske níaddo!

nebri! ambessa!
shla zeíemsemay!

emo barnet aleka!

entay belka?

msla eyu msla abotatka
barya eyu / Hagaziu / zSelíe / ebleka!

Adam, You

Adam,
Son of the sixth day
Of creation,
But no better
Than a slave?

No lion,
No tiger,
No eagle?

You obey
Like an ass,
A mule,
Or a cow—

No better than a slave.
Why not free?

What?
Your ancestors say
That I'm the slave
If I blame you
For helping?

CHARLES CANTALUPO has translated two books of poetry by Reesom Haile, *We Have Our Voice* and *We Invented the Wheel*, and he is the co-translator / editor of *Who Needs a Story? Contemporary Eritrean Poetry in Tigrinya, Tigre and Arabic*. He is also a co-author of the historic Asmara Declaration on African Languages and Literature and the writer / director of the documentary *Against All Odds*, on African language literature. His memoir, *Joining Africa – From Anthills to Asmara*, is a story of poets and poetry in Africa. HIs new book of poetry, *Where War Was – Poems and Translations of Poems from Eritrea* includes new translations of poems by Reesom Haile.

አይተጣዕሱን

አዳምን ሄዋንን
ገነት አይተመልሱን
አይተጣዕሱን

አዳም ሓወይ
እንቋዕ ተረፈና
ዝሃበና ን'ቅበል
እንስሳ ዲና?

ሄዋን ሓብተይ
ዝወሸከሉ እንተሎ
ዝርሃጽክሉ እንጌራ
ዘመሰሉዎ ዶ'ሎ?

አዳምን ሄዋንን
ገነት አይተመልሱን
አይተጣዕሱን

No Regrets

Forget Eden.
We're not going back.
Adam and Eve
Had no regrets.

"Good riddance,"
She said.
"So we were fed.
He treated us like animals.
Adam, I love you."

"I love you, too,"
He said.
"Nothing beats bread
Baked with your sweat."

Forget Eden.
We're not going back.
Adam and Eve
Had no regrets.

CHIKA UNIGWE

Heart of Darkness

T HE DAY I MET Conrad, he rescued a snake about to be eaten by a tiger on his way to school. That was why his uniform was dirty. Our class teacher let him off. He did not get five lashes of the cane which was the regular punishment for untidiness. Maybe it was because he was a new student. Maybe our teacher liked the daringness of his excuse. Whatever it was, he got off a lot more lightly than any other student would have imagined possible. Later that day Conrad told me his father was wealthy but that he had died in a car accident on his way back from work earlier that year. Two weeks later he told me his father died in a fire that razed their humongous house and all the money in it. That was why his mother had to move them to a new city and a small house. By then we had become best friends. Even after many years, not even I, privy to his secret crushes and his desire to travel the world, knew where Conrad lived before he moved to our Uwani neighbourhood or how he lost his father. His story changed with each telling.

CHIKA UNIGWE was born and raised in Enugu, Nigeria. She was shortlisted for the Caine Prize in 2004. Her writing awards include a Rockefeller Foundation Fellowship, a UNESCO Ashberg Fellowship, a BBC short story award and a Commonwealth short story award. In 2012, she won the Nigeria Literature Prize for her novel *On Black Sisters Street* (Random House). She now lives and works in Atlanta, Georgia.

Conrad was always turning up late. If he told you he would be at your place at 1 pm, it was safe for you to assume that he would not turn up before 3. Very often he did not offer any apology. When he did it was always something bold, and delivered with a deadpan voice and a straight face as if he was reading out a shopping list. "Aliens abducted me and forced me to peel a huge pile of yams before they would let me go." "I bumped into the ghost of my great-grandfather and he begged me to keep him company." "I helped a pregnant woman deliver her quadruplets." Once when he held a group of us up for an inter-school football match, he told us the taxi he came in had been involved in accident. "I had to be cut free from the car. Better to be late than be late." We could have called him Pino- Pino- Pinocchio like we did liars but we never did. Instead we nicknamed him Conrad the Late, and asked him to elaborate, to put some flesh on the skeleton of the stories he fed us. Sometimes he obliged us. Conrad had a hold on us. He was tall. The tallest boy in our class, not only taller than our headmaster whom we called Shortmandevil but as tall as many of the female teachers by the time we were in primary 4. By primary 5, he had a sprinkling of fine hair over his upper lip. That commanded respect. Perhaps the truth is that although we never acknowledged it, we admired his ability to spin these tales, perhaps even enjoyed them.

Their sheer daringness immunised them against our ridicule. The manner of delivery inspired deference. So, we always forgave Conrad his tales and his lateness. Not everyone did.

Once, Conrad came very late to school. Even by his own standards, he was late. We were in the middle of our second lesson for the day when he came in, his uniform crisp and clean, his school bag hanging from his back. Shortmandevil spied him from his office and followed him into our classroom. When he asked him why he was 'sauntering in' at that time, Conrad said, "Sir, on my way to school I saw a lion at the end of the street. I ran for dear life and did not dare come out again until I saw the lion run past in the opposite direction." The same story he had spun us. In the same manner he had delivered it to us. Face as bland as a bucket of water. Shortmandevil was not impressed and was not as forgiving as we were and gave Conrad a thorough beating with the leather belt reserved for disciplining unruly pupils. Two days later, it was announced on the 9 o'clock news that a lion had escaped from the zoo. Conrad told us that what he had seen was a vision. He started charging classmates 30 kobo to tell their future. The shinier the coin, he said, the better he could see. For the girls, they could make their coins "spiritually shinier" by kissing the back of his hand.

I did not believe him but I never told him. We were best friends. The obligations of friendship mandated my complicity in his game. There was also the way in which Conrad frowned while reading palms that made you think that he believed he had the gift. His thin neck, bent over the palms, lent him an air of fragility so that I believed that any aspersions cast on his ability to see the future—in jest or otherwise—would snap off that neck of his. On his part, as our intimacy demanded, his predictions for me were never bad. He always told me the same thing: "You will move overseas and marry a woman with red lipstick and generous melons like Miss Priscilla."

Miss Priscilla, our class teacher, was the most glamorous woman we had ever seen. She made primary 6 heaven for all 12-year-old boys on the verge of puberty. She wore tight tops which stretched across her chest and showed off her huge breasts. Even now, when I think of Miss Priscilla, I get aroused.

I asked Conrad once what he saw in his own future. He said he could not read his own palm but he knew that his future was golden. He would go abroad. He would make money. He would have many girlfriends. Then after he had sown his wild oats, he would settle down, marry a beautiful woman and have sons to carry on his Obiohia name. As the only son, it fell on him to make sure the father's name did not vanish. Whenever we joked about not having children until we were very old, at least thirty, he would say in the voice of an old man, "My sisters will marry and take on other men's names. The responsibility of keeping the Obiohia name alive depends on me. I'll have to start as soon as possible." The weight of this responsibility made him seem much more grown up than the rest of us. He insisted on being called Mr. Conrad Obiohia at an age when we still wore shorts to school and reserved 'mister' for adults. "Name is identity," he said once when I asked him to stop going on about marriage and sons, and concentrate on the Jackie Chan film we were watching. "Name is identity." I had no idea what he meant. He was always saying things like that. "Love is power." "To be or not to be. Therein lies the dilemma." "The road less travelled is where treasure lies." Aphorisms that he must have collected from his mother, an English lecturer at the polytechnic.

After we left secondary school, Conrad moved to Lagos. He was done with school, he said. It was time for him to give his future a chance "to unravel," as if his future were a tight ball of wool. The last time I saw him, he told me, "Ejike, my future begins now. I am off to build my business empire."

Conrad's first postcard to me came 4 years after I saw him last. It was a picture of a castle in water, coloured lights bouncing off the water. It looked like a scene from a film.

On the back, Conrad scrawled,

Ejike nwoke m,
Turnhout by night. This is where I live. It's a city shaped like a dog standing

on its hind legs. The statue in the water is an exact replica of my amazon of a woman. Check out the melons on her! I wish you were here, my friend. Here too enjoying life in this beautiful city. Remember, Experience is not what happens to a man. It is what a man does with what happens to him – Aldous Huxley
Conrad Obiohia

I did not even know that he had left the country. I turned the card over to see the statue that I had missed, stunned as I was by the mesmerizing vision of the house on water. It was a huge woman, generously endowed, lying on her side. All her features seemed exaggerated, designed to draw attention to her voluptuousness. I had never heard of Turnhout and scanned the stamp closely for clues of which country it had come from. Belgium. What was Ejike doing in Belgium? Trading in cars? No one I knew had been to Belgium. Abroad was London and America. And these days, South Africa and even Ghana. Or if you got a Catholic scholarship, Cuba or Ukraine. Belgium did not exist for us except as a synonym for the secondhand cars flooding the Tokunbo market. My trusted car was a Japanese-made Belgium. It still bore the sticker of De Rode Duivels it had when I bought it. I knew De Rode Duivels even if the only international matches I watched were the ones played at Old Trafford.

Two weeks later, another card came from him. This time the photograph was of a modern building with the statue of a small man Conrad referred to as "the Prof" in front of it. "De Warande" was printed in block letters across the house. On the back of the card, Conrad wrote:

Ejike nwoke m,
This is my vacation house. People here have vacation houses the same

way we have second homes in the village. The "Prof" is my wife's great-great-great grandfather. He was the 1st man to perform open heart surgery in this country. Luckily he had the good sense to marry a woman far taller than he was. He is said to have come up only to his wife's waist. She too had amazing melons. It is to her that I owe my wife's size. I am having a brilliant time here. Enjoying life.

Never forget: True heroism consists in being superior to the ills of life, in whatever shape they may challenge us to combat: Bonaparte

Conrad Obiohia

The next card arrived less than two weeks later. Across the photograph of a sculpture was inscribed, Adam and Eva. The sculpture was of a couple entwined so tightly that it was difficult to tell where one ended and the other began. It was as if they flowed into each other. Hands, legs, buttocks. It looked like a massive trunk.

Ejike my friend,

This is a very famous artwork. People from all over Belgium come to Turnhout to admire this. It was made by my amazon's mother. Talent and genius run in their family. You reckon Eve had such impressive melons?

The sculpture is a temple to naturists. They come and worship at its feet. Also women who have difficulty getting pregnant come here on pilgrimage. All they have to do is rub their palms over Adam's tight buttocks 10 times, go home, sleep with their men and bingo!

I am having the time of my life here nwoke m. I am happy. Surrounded by people.

Remember: It's better to have loved and lost than never to have loved at all:
Alfred Lord Tennyson.
   Conrad O.

Every few weeks another postcard would come. He had stopped signing the cards with his last name and after a few weeks, the O. disappeared too and he signed off simply as Con. For as long as I had known him, he had never abbreviated his name. It was also around this time that he told me that he was writing a novel, "an epic that will revolutionise the way critics and readers think of the Novel. The mother of all novels. It'll be about my life here, about immigration, about migrants, about my discovery." I always thought that Conrad missed his calling. He should have been a writer. But in primary school, when we all enjoyed writing English compositions, Conrad found them a chore. Perhaps his imagination rebelled at being defined, so that an essay to write two pages on "What I Would Do if I Won 5 Million Naira" was an exercise in torture for this boy who held us spellbound for hours telling the most thrilling stories. Our Primary 5 English composition teacher would have been pleased to know that he was writing a novel. Each time Conrad came up with an excuse of why his homework was late, the teacher would tell him gravely that "a mind was a terrible thing to waste." That with such imagination as he had he would make a fantastic author. "I do not want to be a writer. You're right. A mind is a terrible thing to waste," was Conrad's confident default response.

Conrad never included a return address so I could not write back to him. I could have asked his mother who still lived in the same house in Uwani but I figured that if he wanted me to respond, he would not have omitted his address. Conrad was deliberate like that. Even with his stories. He measured what he said, carefully, like a meat seller weighing meat. He never gave more than he intended to. His moving to Turnhout, this place nobody else had ever heard of, was also most likely a calculated choice, not a random decision picked by fate.

His stories fascinated me. At the beginning, I looked up the names of the places he mentioned on Google search, looking for what he might be hiding, clues to why he had chosen to settle in that city. But every time Google spat out the truth about Turnhout, about the buildings, about the sculptures on the postcard, it depressed me with its truthfulness. The truth was precise. Dry. Detailed. It left no room for wonderment, did not keep me amused, so I stopped seeking it out but stuck instead to Conrad's version.

Once he sent a card with people walking through what was obviously a shopping street. They all had paper bags and some clutched children or carried dogs. Conrad wrote that they were all walking through his private driveway after a birthday party for his wife. And the paper bags I could see were filled with party favours. Another time, he sent me a card of a place called Begijnhof. On the card, a church and a narrow, cobbled road were visible. He said that Begijnhof was the last name of his wife and her great grandfather had placed every stone on that road by hand. To show their gratitude, the city named the area after him. His stories were never the same but they always ended with him saying what a great life he was living. Always.

From his postcards, I could sketch Turnhout, this city I had never seen, in a country I had never been to. I could tell you it had a restaurant called Hof Ter Duine (Conrad's wife's family owned it); it had a big cathedral (St. Peter's, in which he and his amazon got married); De Herentalstraat (where the bakery he always got bread from was: Guylicx. Named after his wife). In the spring flowers bloomed like in the Hollywood films we watched; the old lived in care homes even if they had children who could care for them, people pushed their dogs in prams like babies and on a street called Gildenstraat, a woman lived who spoke to elves and fairies. Conrad said he had started writing. Sometimes the cards said nothing. At other times the stories were disjointed as if Conrad could not decide what to write to me about. But I delighted in receiving them all.

I got so used to the postcards that when they suddenly stopped coming I missed them. At first, I would check my mailbox as soon as I got in from work and if there was no card from Conrad I would get the same hollow feeling in my stomach as if I were hungry. After a month, I started checking my mailbox twice a week. After three months, I no longer opened it with eager anticipation and I no longer felt the emptiness like a hunger in my stomach when my hopes were dashed. In his own good time, he would get back in touch, I thought.

In the year that he wrote to me, Conrad never sent me a photograph. Not of him. Not of his amazon. Or of the children he said he had (twins: a boy and a girl with eyelashes like a giraffe's). I was certain, they were nothing more than figments of his imagination. Yet I read the cards, I imagined his life in a castle with a woman with enormous melons and the twins who called him Papa and sucked their thumbs identically.

I soon forgot about Conrad and it was two years before I thought of him again. I was married and had a son of my own. Holding my son, I felt a longing for my oldest friend, the one who always dreamed of sons. I had been twice to Europe in the six months since he was born. Once to England and once to Holland. Both times I was told Belgium was just a train ride away. "Small country. Like a handkerchief. I'm sure it wouldn't take you much time to find your friend," one of my Dutch colleagues joked when I told him about Conrad living in Belgium. I wished I had an address so that I could have gone over to see him.

To be so close yet so far.

Often I would bring out his cards and scan them for clues of where he lived. Maybe he had left Turnhout. Perhaps even left Belgium. Maybe he lived somewhere else. Two years was a long time. Who was to say that he hadn't even returned to Nigeria like he predicted for himself all those many years ago. Occasionally I googled him but I never got any match. If he had published his novel, there was no trace of it. But it delighted me to think that he might be hard at work on it. Putting that brilliant creative mind of his to good use. Then slowly he receded again to the back of my mind to join other clutter: books read but no longer thought of; I no longer thought of him walking the cobbled streets of Turnhout. I no longer imagined him admiring the melons on Eve and the amazon in the water. Life took over. I had first one son, then another. When I had a third son, I imagined I was living the dream Conrad had all those years ago; to have a house full of sons to perpetuate his father's name. This thought came up one night, the second day after my son's birth while I held him and smelt the newness of him. The thought stayed with me all through the week, buzzing in my ears like an annoying fly. When I could not shake it off after two weeks, I walked to Conrad's mother's house. Even though I had hoped she would still be there, I was shocked to find that she was.

She could as I had hoped fill me in on Conrad the Late. She spoke in a whisper, as if saying a prayer. Pausing occasionally as if to draw breath, she did not stir from her chair until she was done talking.

Conrad's business venture in Lagos had failed monumentally. His time keeping disability and his tales cost him customers. He was so sure, so certain his future lay in Europe that he invested what money he had into buying his passage. Belgium was a wild-card choice from a man in Badagary who could get his clients passports but Turnhout was a deliberate choice. It had many Africans. A good place to begin again.

At first, Conrad had sent many optimistic letters home, praising the city, its lights, its Africans, its fountains in the city square. He would work hard, make some money and return home to start all over again. "But soon," his mother said, "he began to complain about the loneliness. About being unable to leave before he'd made some money. He hated that he was so poor growing up. When he married he sent home a long letter. He sounded very well. He said a Belgian wife eased things. It did not matter that they did not understand each other." His wife hardly spoke any English. Conrad spoke no Flemish so what conversation they had was made up mostly of gesticulations. At first, it had not mattered. Then the exoticism wore off and it began to grate. His marriage crumbled. His letters became long ramblings on the nature of life and loneliness. He started talking about owning castles and islands. "There was a great darkness in his heart," his mother said. "It ate him up. Over there they called him Sule Ibrahim. His 'asylum' name. His passport said he was a Muslim from Sierra Leone. His file said he was escaping a war. I think that story created for him always bothered him." She paused.

"I wandered lonely as a cloud," she said suddenly. "Do you know the poem?"

"No."

"No one survives solitude."

She pressed a photograph in my hand before I left. She gave it to me face down as if she did not want to startle me by disclosing who was in it. I turned it over. A lump rose in my throat. Staring at me were two toddlers with Conrad's high forehead sucking their thumbs in the same identical way.

Born in Larache, Morocco, in 1961, **HASSAN HAJJAJ** left Morocco for London at an early age. Heavily influenced by the club, hip-hop, and reggae scenes of London as well as by his North African heritage, Hajjaj is a self-taught and thoroughly versatile artist whose work includes portraiture, installation, performance, fashion, and interior design, including furniture made from recycled utilitarian objects from North Africa. Turning to photography in the late 80s, Hajjaj started taking studio portraits of friends, musicians, and artists, as well as strangers from the streets of Marrakech, often wearing clothes designed by the artist. These colorful and engaging portraits combine the visual vocabulary of contemporary fashion photography and pop art, as well as the studio photography of African artist Malick Sidibe, in an intelligent commentary on the influences of tradition on the interpretations of high and low branding, and the effects of global capitalism. The artist lives and works between London and Marrakech.

Hassan Hajjaj,
Poetic Pilgrimage, 2010

ISAAC O. DELANO
Translated from the Yoruba by AKIN ADESOKAN

The Age of White Rulers
(Aye D'Aye Oyinbo)

I: In a Polygamous Home

THOSE BYGONE days, when we were young, we knew a life of pleasures. Peace reigned. Food was plentiful. People lived according to their stations in life. The powerful acted with liberty; they took advantage of their neighbors without fear of consequence. If you were born into a good family, that was your luck; you were free to do as you pleased. No one dared confront you. I, Asabi the Discerning, was a freeborn, an epitome of nobility, and I grew up with a sense of my worth. My father was the commander of our town's army, the Balogun, the title that became his name. Whenever he went to war, he returned with scores of captives. Some of these he sold into slavery, some he sacrificed to Ogun, his

ISAAC O. DELANO was an important Nigerian writer and a foremost man of letters. Equally at home in Yoruba and English, he was praised for "bridging the gap," between the intellectual cultures of both, and he published four novels, two biographies, the first and only Yoruba-Yoruba dictionary, a book of proverbs, and an ethnography-cum-travel memoir entitled *The Soul of Nigeria*. At the time of his death in 1979, Delano was a Senior Research Fellow at the former University of Ife (now Obafemi Awolowo University), Ile-Ife. The novel *Aye D'Aye Oyinbo* is significant in that it offers a counterpoint to the well-known narrative, in modern African letters, about the colonial experience as essentially oppressive.

AKIN ADESOKAN's books include *Roots in the Sky*, a novel, and *Postcolonial Artists and Global Aesthetics*, a critical study.

orisa, the rest he took as wives. Our compound was as busy as a daily market. We children alone numbered up to two dozen, not counting the young slaves, the bonded, and the numerous others who arrived in our house as maidservants to young brides and there found their own husbands.

And my mother? Solabomi the Delicate, death-repellent, the wealthy one who funded strife. Thus did my father hail her every morning, saying her *oriki* as she knelt in greeting before him. He would greet her, griot her, and my mother would grow swollen-headed with pride.

My mother was exceedingly beautiful, slender and dark. She was not a captive, nor was she a bondswoman. After all, the enslaved or the bonded bore no *oriki*, except maybe where they came from. She was married formally; my father paid the bride-price and went through the rituals of betrothal, in the fashion of those days. She was distinguished as a trader in beads and other bodily accessories. Among her wares were bracelets, *segi*, corals, amethysts, and silver earrings. From a special type of ruby the size of a thumb she strung for my father a beaded necklace befitting a high chief. For he was not just the Balogun; he occupied a civil position as well. Bedecked with those rich beads, my father went everywhere with pomp and swagger, proud husband of a woman who knew the worth of appearance. Thus he treated my mother as the trophy wife, to the envy of her co-wives. Naturally, this attitude was extended to me and my siblings, so that my father treated us better than our half-brothers and half-sisters. This preference almost caused a trouble; it nearly turned into a civil strife. The rest of the compound resented us. When neither my father nor his favorite wife was nearby, people snapped their fingers at us saying, "Someday, you will see."

We, my mother's children, were three. One afternoon, Obafunke, the eldest, died suddenly. Obafunke fair of skin, tall and slender, beloved of our parents.

My father in particular doted on him, for he resembled him in appearance. My mother, after all, was of dark complexion. His death saddened my parents to no end; there was widespread belief that it was not a natural death, but the doing of my mother's co-wives. My father believed this talk, and so did my mother. They wept bitterly that day, both of them. For a man, and a titled chief at that, my father's conduct was unbecoming. There he sat, weeping like a woman! Neighbors and friends beseeched him. Such are the ways of Providence, they told him, you must be a man. But he would not be comforted. He would stare into space for a while, then jump to his feet and say:

"Where is my Obafunke? Ha, whoever brought this misfortune on us will leave this world without offspring!"

And another round of wailings would begin. With my mother it was worse. She cried so much her eyeballs grew resentful. She ran to the housefront, threw herself on the ground, writhing in the throes of a great sorrow. Even we, the children, did our share of crying. Our entire compound was one huge noise of bereavement. The news of Obafunke's death spread everywhere, and neighbors came to sympathize with us. They stood by us. It was a sad day for my family.

In the evening, the men of the neighborhood buried Obafunke on a patch in front of our house. As the grave was covered with earth, more people took to crying. In the days that followed, my mother regularly returned to mourn at the graveside at night. She sat there crying and hailing her son, whose death had cast her world adrift. One such night, going to observe her routine, she arrived to find my father already there. Apparently they had both made a habit of visiting the grave, but had never encountered each other until that night. Husband and wife both broke into wailing, of such decibel that it woke up not just the house but the entire neighborhood. It was not a mean affair. Neighbors pleaded with them again, and thereafter the elders called my father in private. Nobody knew what they said to him, but after that day he did not go back to Obafunke's grave to cry.

I was the middle child; my younger brother was named Adekanbi, and Obafunke the eldest had just died. The two remaining children became the apples of our parents' eyes. The affection was exceeding, it was incredible; and even now that I am grown in years, with my own family, it continues to amaze me that a man, my father, who had made a profession of killing people in war and of selling others into slavery, behaved like a woman when it came to his own children. He adored us to the point of affecting our characters. True, the slave and the freeborn come into the world in like manners; but my father treated us with especial care. He truly adored us.

As evidence of this superseding love, our parents decided to protect Adekanbi and me with charms, so we might escape death, avert ill-health, the evil eye of the people of this world; that sorcerers might not set eyes on us, nor witches even look in our direction. We received incisions at every joint in our bodies, charmed rings adorned our necks, and potent waistbands our waists. These they called "insurance," and they treasured those charms most assuredly, because soon enough they caused me to wear anklets in addition. This they explained as the counsel of the Ifa oracle, which had decided that I was a strange child. Regularly our parents made feasts because of us; they would kill a goat, cook beans (as if we were twins!), fry yams and beans and gather children from the neighborhood to eat of the feast. These were great expenses which I did not understand at the time. Even now, as I write of those days, I still do not fully appreciate the love. My parents displayed exceptional love. Surely parents love their children more than children can understand or reciprocate.

Meanwhile, I regarded myself with these accoutrements, going to bed and waking in them. I would stare at Adekanbi for some time and taunt him about his appearance, which reminded me of Fikuyeri, a fearsome masquerade in our neighborhood. Fikuyeri emerged every year festooned with charms to harass children all over the neighborhood. But what about me? What did I look like? Adekanbi found the perfect comparison: Sorowanke. Now Sorowanke was a female lunatic, who dressed herself in junk and brass anklets, and proceeded to dance in the streets. The day they pointed her out to me, and I saw the person to whom I was being likened, I was extremely infuriated. In consequence I yanked off all the junk that my parents had used to "insure" me.

Adekanbi had gone prowling the city. Returning, he was followed by drummers who hailed him with praises, and so he looked exactly like Fikuyeri! I laughed and said, "Fikuyeri, I greet you!"

And the drummers saluted him thus: "Adekanbi, child of Balogun. You will surely measure up to your father!"

I laughed so much I shed tears, but nobody knew why I was laughing. But as he was taking steps in response to the drummers' efforts, Adekanbi looked every inch like Fikuyeri. He clearly did not recognize me upon entering, for he turned to me to inquire about my whereabouts. I smiled quietly now, and delved into a corner. He looked around and could not "see" me. His sight had not quite adjusted to the room; he had been in the scorching sun for a long time. He sweated much, not realizing I was the one standing nearby. Turning to me again, he yelled: "Where is Asabi, that Sorowanke look-alike?" Laughter rose to my neck, but I suppressed it. I saw two kids close by and winked to them to gain their confidence. They laughed, but I continued to keep a straight face. When Adekanbi repeated his question, no one could bear it further, and our collective laughter gave the game away. He now discovered that he had been asking me about me all the while. Stunned, he asked the question a third time. Now I answered him: "Yes, it's me! You, you look like Fikuyeri!"

Breaking into a hooligan's laughter, he started chasing me round the house, hoping to attack me. Adekanbi with his street-boy's ways. Immediately, he began to tear off the charms and amulets strung on his arms and legs. Within moments, he had turned himself into a tall and handsome young man.

It was an unforgettable day in our family. When my father came home and saw that we no longer had our protective charms, he flew into a rage. He did not realize it right away; an entire hour passed after his arrival before he noticed our unusual appearances. This was surprising because my own anklets littered the housefront, and it was from this direction that he had entered. He was outraged. He spoke angrily. He created a scene. He cursed. It was not us he cursed, let me be fair. After all, he treasured me and my brother a lot. He directed much of his anger at my mother; it was she whom he accused of encouraging us to discard the charms. As the father, he said, his own loss would be minimal if we too were to die suddenly, like Obafunke. He had other children. Well, we did not die and we did not take ill; our ancestors watched over us. And who were our ancestors? We knew them in the *egungun*, the masked beings that came from the heavens. To tell you the truth, that day I was terrified of my father's rage. I had never seen him in that mood before. Trust Adekanbi! He laughed through it all, but did so quietly.

On moonlit nights, after supper, we gathered on a platform in the backyard and told stories. Children would make riddles, *aalo*, before telling stories. That was the order of proceeding. Thus the saying: "The riddlemaker who fails to tell stories is a country yokel." On the night that I am talking about, I kicked off the riddle session with the customary preamble. I called out, "Aalo o," and Adekanbi and other children of the compound responded, "Aalo!"

"What passes by the king's palace without acknowledging him?"

"Sorowanke!" replied Adekanbi.

"A fool," said another kid.

"The flood," another one said.

"That's right!" I replied. "It's the flood."

I cannot relate all the events of that night, the sense of relief we channeled into telling riddles and stories to compensate for my father's disappointment at our conduct. The bright full moon turned the night into day; the moon had ripened into its final phase. After a while, the young men brought out their sound-boxes. Thus was our storytellers' gathering dispersed; playing the sound-box was more exciting than storytelling. We undertook these nightly games. The years of childhood were full of memories. There were fine memories during my youth, too. And even now, in my old age, things are not so bad, in spite of the trials I have been through.

When we were young, the elders and even the youth partook of the nightly gatherings. It was only the mothers who hardly ever came out to join the groups, as though they were confined to a harem. They labored without respite. Either they were looking after their young children or they were busy preparing meals for their husbands. The women's lot was miserable in those bygone days.

Time continued on its course. I grew in age, and so did Adekanbi. Everyone weathered time and took on more years. What a strange entity, this thing called time! For this reason, child, do not waste time on any undertaking. For the time which I recall only seems like yesterday. Before I knew it, I had become a young maiden, ready for the ways of womanhood. My mother, Solabomi, often counseled me on the challenges faced by the womenfolk. The life of a woman was delicate; a minor mistake might take years to repair. She advised me on how one conducted oneself in marriage; the do's and the don'ts. These things pertained to how you treat your husband, what you do to curry the favor of your mother-in-law, what is expected of a wife from the family and friends of her husband. My mother spoke about these and other things as well. For instance, she took me into confidence on which of her co-wives liked us and which hated us. Indeed, she secretly whispered to me the name of the person she strongly suspected of killing Obafunke, my brother.

In our compound, my fathers' many wives were not friendly to one another, in spite of the fact that they shared meals and drinks. They attended social functions together, dressed uniformly in *aso-ebi*, as a mark of solidarity. That was for the attention of outsiders; the fellow-feeling was not sincere. In fact, they intensely hated one another. Soon, I too began to discern who my friend was, and who my enemy. I resolved that I would never talk to certain people, particularly the person who I now believed was responsible for my brother's death.

Thus did distrust and intrigue fester in a polygamous family. It is only now that I am advanced in years that these things seem less confusing to me. If I were a man, believe me, I would take no more than one wife on account of my experiences, as a daughter and as a wife. Most of the counsels my mother offered concerned life in a polygamous home. Simply put, it was a struggle. To be even more exact, it was the kind of struggle that required deep intelligence. But she also initiated me into other kinds of struggle, like the business of trading. I joined her in selling her wares, went with her to the market where she bought the goods. It became clear to me that trading, what we call buying-and-selling, was difficult work. However, I excelled in it, and my father provided me with the start-off funds.

At this time, many young men began to trouble me; they wanted to marry me. I was attracted to the dark-skinned, to the light-skinned, and to the tall ones. How I detested short men! I counted it as a supreme blemish. I was giddy with these attentions, and could not make up my mind. I often expressed these frustrations to my mother; after all, a maiden's mother is her first confidant.

She said, "A hasty marriage leaves you without one in the end. Men aren't like that."

Those words were pregnant, too complex for me at the time. But now I know. Anyone who fails to carefully choose a wife or husband will regret it in the end. On my way to the market, a man would ambush me. While returning home, another would hail me. I did not blame them; I was beautiful, and was conscious of it. I moved with grace, walked with a swagger. It was my time, after all.

One morning, early at dawn, my father called me into his room.

"Asabi, my child, the Discerning," he said. "Your life shall be happy, you shall prosper…I have found a man for you."

I said, "Found a man for me?"

"Yes," he replied.

"Have I cried to you about needing a husband? An earthly husband or a ghostly one?"

It was disrespectful to talk to my father in such a jesting tone, but I was already quite furious. And who was the man that he had found for me? His name was Babalola, the eldest son of the chief of the maskers in our town. When he said this, I laughed in derision, forgetting that I was before an elder, and launched into another jest.

"Did I ask you to find a man for me? Well, I already found myself a man. He is the son of Efun, the Obatala priestess."

My father too laughed, but he did not look amused. He was frowning. Anger was visible on his face.

Said he, "That will not be. Is that what you and your mother are plotting? No way!"

It seemed like a joke, and we jested about it, but gradually that morning the matter developed into rancor. Why would the mother be blamed for her child's conduct? I wondered about this at the time, and even now, I still do not understand why my mother was to be blamed for my actions. My father remained obstinate about his proposition, as he was certain that my mother was my counselor and had a hand in my disobedient attitude. I was as resolute in my decision to marry the Obatala priestess's son.

My mother camped nearby, eavesdropping on the debacle. She did not put in a word. After all, in those days, a woman did not have much of a say in the things that concerned her child. But thereafter, she called me in private, and warned me against talking to my father in such a disrespectful manner in the future. She advised me to follow his wishes, saying a solid family home was as important as a good matrimonial home, for marriage was not a minor matter. Further, she advised me to apologize to him the following morning, to make up for my insolent behavior. Of course, I refused. Now I can see clearly where I was wrong. I was not just being rude to my father; I had also committed to the priestess's son, and I really liked him. Obviously my father had got wind of that before he called me in that morning. Love could be blind.

ZANELE MUHOLI

"Massa" and Minah

ZANELE MUHOLI is a South African photographer and visual activist whose work explores gender, race, and sexuality, particularly in relation to South African society and the political landscape. In 2009, Muholi wrote a thesis mapping the visual history of black lesbian identity and politics in post-Apartheid South Africa as part of her MFA in Documentary Media from Ryerson University, Toronto. Since 2004 Muholi has exhibited extensively worldwide, most recently at the Brooklyn Museum (NYC). She has also taken part in important exhibition platforms such as the 55th Venice Biennale and Documenta 13 in Kassel. She is the recipient of numerous prizes and one of the shortlisted photographers for the 2015 Deutsche Börse Prize for her seminal series, *Faces and Phases*.

Massa and Minah I,
2008

Massa and Minah VI, 2010

(Facing page) Massa and Maids IV, 2009

Massa and Minah II, 2008

Massa and Minah III, 2008

Minah V, 2009

KERRY BYSTROM

Queer(y)ing Domestic Service

S INCE SOUTH AFRICA'S "liberation" in 1994, much has changed, and much has remained the same. This is certainly the case with the institution of domestic service. Having a domestic worker is no longer the almost exclusive domain of the white upper and middle classes but common among wealthy people of all races, and many master-servant relationships have taken new directions. Yet attitudes of white paternalism deeply engrained during apartheid persist, alongside a kind of willed blindness to the costs for workers themselves of the "intimate labor" extracted through an exploitative system that treats them "like family" rather than as normal employees. As domestic worker Joyce Nhlapo noted in 2009, "inside white people's houses, it is still apartheid law. We are their servants, like girls. You have grandchildren, but you are still their 'girl.'"

Zanele Muholi's on-going photographic series "'Massa' and Minah," from which the images here are drawn, stands as a challenge to such lines of continu-

KERRY BYSTROM teaches English and Human Rights at Bard College Berlin. She is the author of *Democracy at Home in South Africa: Family Fictions and Transitional Culture* and co-editor, with Sarah Nuttall, of the special issue of *Cultural Studies* "Private Lives and Public Cultures in South Africa".

ity and a provocation to think differently about domestic work and domestic workers. These images depict Muholi herself posed in scenes—both realistic and fantastical—drawn from her memories and imagination of the life of her mother Bester Muholi. As the artist describes it for the Stevenson gallery where a selection of these images were first exhibited in 2009:

> In . . . "Massa" and Mina(h) (2008), I turn my own black body into a subject of art. I allow various photographers to capture my image as directed by me. I use performativity to deal with the still racialized issues of female domesticity— black women doing house work for white families. The project is based on the life and story of my mother. I draw on my own memories, and pay tribute to her domesticated role as a (domestic) worker for the same family for 42 years. The series is also meant to acknowledge all domestic workers around the globe who continue to labour with dignity, while often facing physical, financial, and emotional abuses in their place of work. There continues to be little recognition and little protection from the state for the hard labour these women perform to feed and clothe and house their families.

Since 2009, Muholi has continued adding images to the series. The "tribute" and call for "acknowledgement" Muholi articulates can be seen clearly in images such as "Massa and Minah II," which renders visible both the tough labor accomplished by domestic workers and its disregard by those socially and literally higher placed. The need for "recognition" and "protection" takes center stage in "Massa and Minah VI," where the character Minah pauses in her duties to turn away from the camera in a moment of anxiety or distress, and "Minah V," where she inhabits a room barren of personal detail and sits in an awkward position that underscores a kind a bodily discomfort and sense of smallness. Again she stares away from the camera, filled with thoughts of somewhere or someone else. Is she a live-in maid and this her living quarters? How often can she go home? Is she thinking of her children, whom she left to care for her employer's family? And what memories haunt Muholi's pose from within, doubling the maid's isolation with that of a child wishing for her mother?

Muholi's images also stretch the definition of a conventional memorial and the serious aesthetics of much activist art; as curator Gabi Ngcobo reminds us, "[b]y performing the same role as her mother, Muholi makes a chain of gestures including but not limited to that of paying tribute to her mother." This is accomplished in part by Muholi's willingness to play with tonal register, combining images of pain and loss with indignation, self-knowingness, and dark humor to open up new frames for thinking about domestic service. "Massa and Maids IV" satirically inverts the unfortunately all-too-common story of a white master sexually abusing his black domestic worker with an image depicting a man all but worn out by the prowess of his maids. These women are clearly triumphant, radiating control, having found a way to turn the tables on their employer. And yet, on what terms have they won the game? Here as in "Massa and Minah III," there is something deliberately troubling about the way satire re-inscribes (even in reversal) longer narratives about gender, race, and sex in the colonial and apartheid context, making the laughter provoked by the image multiply disruptive.

Queer theory has taught us to be attentive to these shifts across tonal registers, and it is not surprising—especially given Muholi's very public identity as a lesbian photographer—that another way Muholi moves beyond paying tribute is by building into this series the signs of queer desire. Ngcobo writes that the "'Massa' and Minah" images "build up a story of an emerging love affair" between the black maid and white madam depicted there. Desire infuses images such as "Massa and Minah I," with its intimate caress, but this desire across unequal racial and class positions leads to troubles animating all of the images that follow, creating new and intersecting layers of interpretation. What drives desire founded in servitude and what are its emotional impacts? How much agency can Minah have in this situation? Can love alter the power relations between employee, lover, and the family she serves, or it impossible to escape the racialized and socially-reinforced roles of master and servant?

Muholi is most widely known for her work depicting the struggles of black lesbians in South Africa, with earlier projects such as Only Half the Picture documenting hate crimes suffered by this group even as her images seek to enlarge the space for living and loving supposedly guaranteed by the equality laws included in South Africa's 1996 constitution. Xavier Livermon, noting the danger faced by queer black bodies in the democratic state, speaks of the importance of cultural activists "queer(y)ing" a "freedom" that is at best incomplete, whether we speak about freedom from apartheid racism, from heterosexism, or from material want. Borrowing his pun, we might say that Muholi's images productively "queer(y)" domestic service—drawing attention to previously ignored experiences of lesbians within the institution, while at the same time calling for a very needed reexamination of its parameters and place in society as a whole.

Works Cited

Ally, Shireen. *From Servants to Workers: South African Domestic Workers and the Democratic State*. Ithaca: Cornell University Press, 2009.

Bystrom, Kerry. *Democracy at Home in South Africa: Family Fictions and Transitional Culture*. New York: Palgrave MacMillan, 2015.

Muholi, Zanele. "Artist's Statement." Stevenson, 2009. http://www.stevenson.info/exhibitionsbs/muholi/text.htm.

Ncgobo, Gabi. "It's Work as Usual: Framing Race, Class and Gender through a South African Lens." *AfricAvenir,* 2010. http://www.africavenir.org/publications/e-dossiers/revisions/gabi-ngcobo.html.

Livermon, Xavier. "Queer(y)ing Freedom: Black Queer Visibilities in Postapartheid South Africa." *GLQ* 18.2–3 (2012): 297–323.

UNGULANI BA KA KHOSA

Translated by DAVID BROOKSHAW

Ualalapi

UNGULANI BA KA KHOSA's *Ualalapi* won Mozambique's National Prize for Fiction in 1990. It is a collection of six loosely related stories focusing on the figure of Ngungunyane, the emperor of Gaza, who extended his power over much of Southern and Central Mozambique between 1884 and 1895, the year when he was eventually defeated and captured by the Portuguese, who sent him into exile in the Azores, where he died in 1906. After the independence of Mozambique in 1975, the figure of Ngungunyane was rehabilitated, and his remains returned to his native land, where he became a national hero. Among the peoples he suppressed, however, there is an oral tradition surrounding the emperor, which represents him as a brutal tyrant rather than a hero. Khosa tapped this tradition to give us a narrative which could almost be described as a novel, tracing as it does the ruler's rise to power over his murdered rivals and his eventual decline. The six stories are intercalated with excerpts from the writings of colonial officials

You are Ngungunyane!...
You will terrify women and men! . . .
(Anonymous, 19th Century)

WHEN THEY reached one of the small elevations overlooking the nearby village, the warriors sighed with relief as they gazed at the houses scattered among the ancient trees, immersed in a deep silence, typical of that time of day, when the sun had majestically passed its zenith in the cloudless sky, casting its rays mercilessly down on the faces, the backs and the naked torsos of the warriors, sheathed from their waists to the upper part of their thighs in the skins of wild animals.

At the head of his warriors, Ualalapi ran his eyes over the village and thought of the *doro*, the term used to describe the sorghum liquor prepared in these lands of the Mundau, taken to wash down a good chunk of meat in the shade of the leafy tree, while his wife stoked the fire in front of him and his son played, and night fell peacefully, bringing with it the half moon and yet farther away the voices of other men gathered for the evening, their stories journeying over the deeds of the Nguni in times of war and peace.

He smiled at the warriors who accompanied him, loaded down with fresh meat, the result of the slaughter carried out within these lands, and began the descent down a winding path, oblivious to the ceaseless rustling of the tall bushes on either side, until, half-way down, he paused, forcing the others to stop and gather round him.

Two pangolins, creatures of ill omen, gleamed sleepily in the sun, there in the middle of the path. Ualalapi glanced surreptitiously at the warriors on either side of him and detected the same clear, fearful, absent glint in their eyes. He said nothing. He passed his hand over the fresh meat, a sign of abundance and good augury, and then looked hard at the pangolins, animals of ill fortune, as already mentioned. And all of them stood there without moving, as if petrified by the mournful sight, and feeling the sun scorching their bodies and the bushes brushing their most robust branches against them, bending on contact with their bodies, until, after minutes on end, the pangolins regained their strength and withdrew from the path, allowing the men to pass freely and all their sinister thoughts to disperse.

Ualalapi thought of his son and saw him take his shield from so many battles down from the mud-smeared wall. But why his son, he thought, and not the mother of his son who always offered him her body on moonlit nights and on occasions that were sometimes inappropriate for fornication?... He passed his hand through his hair, picked the leaf of a wild plant out of it, looked up at the birds that flew quietly overhead, and felt a slight tremor run through his body. No, it can't be her, he thought, I left her healthy in both body and spirit. And as

involved in the campaign against Ngungunyane. The final episode, which includes the emperor's prophetic speech as he boards the ship for exile, foresees the apocalyptic civil war, which brought the newly independent Mozambique to its knees between 1978 and 1992. The book is a disguised warning against tyranny. "Ualalapi", the first story in the book, recounts Ngungunyane's rise to power following the death of his father, Muzila.

DAVID BROOKSHAW is Professor of Luso-Brazilian Studies at Bristol University, UK and has translated a number of books by Mia Couto, including most recently *Sleepwalking Land* (2006), and *A River Called Time* (2009). He has also compiled an anthology of stories by the Portuguese writer José Rodrigues Miguéis titled *The Polyhedric Mirror: Tales of American Life*, and translated stories of immigrant life in North America by the Portuguese/Azorean/New England writer Onésimo Almeida, *Tales from the Tenth Island*, both of which were published in 2006.

a woman, an Nguni woman, she could foresee her fate. My son as well, that's impossible, for how can the child of Nguni parents die unexpectedly at the age of two, without having been trained in the use of arms like his fathers and grandfathers?... No, it just cannot be that the winds of misfortune will reach the family so soon. It might be the case with these warriors, he thought, and he watched them, their heads hung as if they feared the earth would swallow them up, as they stumbled and tripped over every tiny obstacle. No, it's not these either, for they belong to the masses, and unhappiness has always presented itself to the masses, since the beginning of time, without riddles, as straightforward as their banal lives that have no history or destiny unless to serve their betters until death. So to whom is this puzzle directed if the only family I have is a wife and child? . . . He looked at his warriors and saw that they were in a similar state of recollection, thinking of their wives and children, or their parents and grandparents, while they were being cast out into the boundless empire.

While they were thinking about this and that, recalling both past and present matters related to the mysteries nature mercilessly throws at men, they quickened their step toward the nearby village, whose little streets were deserted, quiet except for the growing murmur of the leaves in the trees and the haphazard wafting of smoke from some of the huts, where fire clung obstinately to the logs as they succumbed to ash.

They grew close to the first hut and Ualalapi went ahead. A middle-aged woman, seated in front of the house, was suckling a child.

"What's wrong, mother?" Ualalapi asked, crouching down and putting his spear down where his right hand could reach it.

"The bats kept flying over the houses, squeaking all the time and bringing spirits to trouble our minds that had long been at rest, and some died," replied the woman with a tired air, as she concerned herself with her child who was desperately moving his feet and eyes, trying to fend off the flies that persisted in settling on him.

"Has anyone in your family died?"

"My husband."

"I'm so sorry, mother... I'm so sorry. And the menfolk, where are the menfolk?"

"Who has the courage to go out and about in these times?... They're consulting their soothsayers. It's not a man who's died but the empire."

"Who else has died?"

"You'll find out. Chiefs like you are awaiting Mudungazi in the square."

"Very well. What did your husband die of?"

"Of fright. But how significant is the ant before the elephant?"

"How many times has the ant not killed the elephant, mother?"

"And how many times has the crocodile left the water, young man?"

"Thank you, mammy," said Ualalapi, perturbed. He got to his feet, grabbed his spear and turned to his warriors who were looking at him, tired of waiting.

"Guard the meat and await orders. I'm going to the square," and he left them without further delay, walking swiftly and oblivious to the wind that gusted grains of sand and scattered leaves, forming little eddies that swirled upwards in chaotic circles, forever touching Ualalapi's body, covered by a layer of blood and bits of leaves. These were detached by the strength of the wind carrying with it a strange smell, first sensed in a long forgotten age when men from other tribes watched the houses swaying in the force of the wind and rain that covered the earth and bushes with pungent, muddy water at the very moment when they had completed the burial of a king of Manica who, as predicted by his *swikiro* – the term Shona people used to describe their spirit mediums – had not ruled for more days than the fingers of his hands. But this had proved time enough for him to grow fat on delicious meals that came to an end on the fateful day when he died of congestion.

By now, Ualalapi was approaching the square, the place where the king's body lay stretched out inside a hut, under the watchful eyes of the kingdom's elders, encharged with the duty of witnessing the corpse's putrefaction so that malevolent spirits should not take possession of bits of the body, and enduring for days and nights the unbearable smell of rotting flesh, the liquids which dripped into receptacles positioned for that purpose. Ualalapi placed his hand over his nose as he entered the square. He looked up at the sky and saw the dark, heavy clouds descending from the heights. The wind buffeted both the loftiest and the shortest trees. He walked up to Mputa, a warrior destined to die a stupid, innocent death, but whose face would remain in everyone's memory. All this was confirmed when his destiny was predicted, although the causes of his death were never explained, for in stories of kings and queens, even the all-prophesying *swikiros* omit such details.

"What's happening, Mputa?"

"Muzila has died."

"How?"

"They say he died of an illness, for he hadn't stopped staring at the ceiling for some nights."

"An inhuman death for an Nguni."

"There are some who say his father died in the same way."

"It wasn't what they wanted, Mputa."

"I know of few kings who have died in battle."

"But they all insist it's the best way to die."

"When they're addressing their warriors."

"You're a very quick thinker."

"That's what war teaches us, Ualalapi."

"You're right... Can you smell this stench?"

"It's the stench of death. When a king dies, some of his subjects are supposed to keep him company."

"I spoke to a woman who lost her husband."

"Others died. When old Salama heard of the king's death, she went to the riverbank and waited for her crocodile ancestors to come and fetch her half an hour after she'd sat down to contemplate the waters of the river. Old Lucere died while he was taking an afternoon nap, devoured by giant ants that didn't leave a trace of the old man's flesh. When Chichuaio stepped inside his house, he found himself surrounded by snakes that fought each other for possession of his body. And there are more cases, it's always like that."

"I know, but it's incredible... How long have you been waiting for Mudungazi?"

"Ever since early afternoon. This smell is too much..."

"It's of those who've long since died, Mputa."

"Bones don't smell, Ualalapi."

"But the spirits can make anything happen."

"You're right. Let's get up. Mudungazi is going to appear. How did the hunt go?"

"It went well. We've got a lot of meat."

"Abundance in the midst of disaster."

"Exactly," said Ualalapi, wiping his body. The clouds threatening the village began to disperse, bearing with them the wind and the stench of death that hovered over the village during the week Ualalapi spent in the interior of the territory of Manica.

II

In a hesitant, mawkish voice, but one which gathered strength as the speech progressed, as is the case with those skilled in the art of addressing the people, Mudungazi began his speech to his warrior chiefs by affirming that matters of the plains had no end. "There are countless harvests that we have conquered with our blood-soaked spears and our shields weary of protecting us.

"We have won battles. We have opened up paths. We have sown corn in stony soil. We have brought rain to these arid lands and we have educated these people, brutalized by the most primitive customs. And today, this people dwell among you, Nguni!

"This empire without limit was built by my grandfather after countless battles in which he was always triumphant. Within it, he spread order and the new customs we brought with us. And when he died, he appointed Muzila, my father, as his successor. Muzila had the heart of a man. He was generous. And many took advantage of his goodness. Among them Mawewe, his brother, who in the midst of shameful intrigue, managed to usurp power without the agreement of the spirits and the grandees of the kingdom who had accepted Muzila as the successor, for it was he who had been the first to prepare the grave where his father would be laid to rest for ever and ever. But Mawewe forgot all this and took the throne for a period of time that history will not record, and if it does, it will do so in order to brand the face of that man I dare not call uncle with the stamp of perfidy.

"At that time, dear warriors, the land was covered with the bodies of innocent folk and the waters took on the tinge of blood for week after week, causing people to drink the blood of their dead brothers because they could no longer bear the thirst that tormented them. And all this because of Mawewe's obstinacy in keeping himself in power.

"Muzila has died, dear warriors. As he lay dying, he appointed me as his successor. His grave should be prepared by me. Do you think history is going to be repeated?"

The warriors, in precise rhythm, beat their leather shields on the ground and shouted "no."

"You are with me," Mudungazi said, "not out of fidelity to me, but because you have respected my words. That is what I expected of you."

He paused in his speech for a few moments, and ran his bloody gaze over his silent warriors. The sun was sinking. The wind was placid. White clouds covered the dark ones in the blue sky.

"My brother, Mafemane," he continued, "lives some fifteen kilometers from here. I am certain that he is getting ready to leave in order to prepare my father's grave. History must not be repeated. Power belongs to me. No one, but no one can take it from me until I die. The spirits have descended into me and are accompanying me, and are guiding me in my wise, well-considered actions. And I shall not allow the same carnage as took place when Muzila took the throne, because I shall act immediately. The men who do not yet know me, will come to know me. I shall not share power. It has belonged to me ever since I was born from the belly of Iozio, my mother, Muzila's favourite wife. And all shall fear me, because I shall not be called Mudungazi, but Ngungunyane, just like those deep furnaces where we hurl those who are condemned to death! Fear and terror of my empire will last for century after century, and it will be heard of in lands that you cannot even dream of! That is why you must sharpen your spears, my warriors. We must clear the path ahead of us with all urgency, so that we don't stumble into possible traps." And so Mudungazi finished his speech to his warriors. Night was now falling. Followed by his aunt, Damboia, Mudungazi walked towards the great hut, his ample flesh swaying, flesh that would change little until the time he died in unknown waters, wrapped in clothes he had always rejected and among people the colour of skinned goat, who had been thoroughly alarmed when they had first set eyes on a black man.

III

"You're in the habit of climbing trees by their branches, Mudungazi."

"They got the message, Damboia."

"I doubt it."

"You only show a warrior his target."

"So why didn't you pick the man to carry out the execution?"

"I'll do that at daybreak. And don't worry about Mafemane: the vultures are already preparing to devour him. Let us take some *doro* to mark my rise to power in this empire."

"To your health, Ngungunyane."

"Indeed, Ngungunyane. I shall be known as Ngungunyane for ever more, and I shall live to a great age. That is what the spirits decreed."

"What's happening, Ualalapi?"

"Muzila has died."

"I know. But what did Mudungazi say?"

"Mafemane must die."

"Why?"

"Only one man should go through the door at a time."

"And the other has to wait outside."

"Ah... men always avoid turning their backs on someone. It's dangerous."

"Not always. But who is going to kill him?"

"You're very worried. Forget it. Is the water for my bath ready?"

"It's warming on the fire. This situation makes me anxious."

"Why?"

"I had strange dreams."

"That's normal when one's in mourning."

"I dreamed of your death."

"My death?"

"Yes."

"How did I die in your dream?"

"You died as you walked along. Your voice sustained your lifeless body. Your son and I died, drowned by the tears that wouldn't stop flowing from our eyes."

"That's incredible, but none of that is going to happen, woman."

"I'm scared, Ualalapi. I'm scared. I can see lots of blood, blood that came from our forefathers who invaded these lands, while their sons and grandsons remain here, killing as well. Blood, Ualalapi, blood! We live on the blood of these innocent people. Why, Ualalapi?..."

"It's necessary, woman. We are a people chosen by the spirits to spread order through these lands. That's why we advance from victory to victory. And before green shoots appear, this land needs to be irrigated with blood. But for the time being you shouldn't worry about anything, because we are in a time of peace and of mourning."

"And what about your brothers, Mudungazi?"

"Which ones?... How. Who, Anyane, Mafabaze?"

"Yes."

"They won't have the courage to go against my orders. The danger lies with Mafemane. He's the one who should die."

"If you're the one chosen to kill Mafemane, refuse, Ualalapi."

"It won't necessarily be me. But why?"

"I fear for your life, Ualalapi."

"Don't worry. I shall only die in combat like my father, who with four spears buried in his chest, was brave enough as only he could be to hurl the spear that I now use at the chest of a Tsonga some ten meters away. I shall only die in combat, woman. It's my fate, and the fate of all the great Nguni warriors."

"Don't deceive yourself, Ualalapi. Many were the warriors who died stupidly and not in battle. Sereko, who killed so many in combat, was killed by a snake sent him by his irate grandfather. Makuko died in the bush, defecating non-stop for two whole weeks. And when they found him, already dead, shit was still coming out of his body. They had to bury him still shitting. You can't get away from this. Men die outside the field of battle. And I'm scared, Ualalapi."

"You're dreaming, woman."

"And how often have my dreams been wrong?"

"You may be right, but if I'm to die, how can I escape my fate?"

"Don't say such things. You exasperate me. What I'm asking is that you should refuse the order to kill Mafemane."

"I owe my loyalty to Mudungazi."

IV

The sun hadn't yet burnt off the dew when Manyune and the warriors under his command drew near Mafemane's village, and began to listen for signs of movement. But the huts of Mafemane and his men and women were shrouded in silence, the same silence that affected everyone during those days. In the narrow streets there was nothing to be seen except for little leaves and bits of broken pots scattered across the ground. Manyune left most of his warriors there and took two with him to Mafemane's house, which stood in the middle of the village. There was something terrifying about that silence, for as they walked towards the heart of the village, the only sound they heard was that of their bare feet treading on the damp ground. Mafemane was awaiting them, standing tall and unflappable in front of his house, his hands crossed on his strong, wide chest.

"I've been expecting you," said Mafemane, walking towards Manyune. "I know that Muzila has died. I also know that my brother has been chosen as his successor, even though I am the eldest son of Fussi, Muzila's first wife. The throne belongs to Mudungazi. I know, too, that you have come with orders to kill me. I am ready to die. But I ask that I should be allowed to say farewell to my wives and children. Come back at the end of the day."

The words came from on high, and penetrated the mind of Manyune and his warriors with such clarity that they were petrified by Mafemane's calmness and serenity. The latter smiled and stared at them. His eyes were transparent, glowing, formidable. Incapable of giving an answer, Mudungazi's men began to retreat, their eyes fixed on Mafemane. Manyune stumbled, fell, got up and turning his back on Mafemane, began to walk so fast that the warriors who were waiting for him were surprised and disturbed.

"What's wrong, Manyune?"

"Don't ask me anything. Let's go, let's go back to our village."

And he led the way. When they got back to their village, they tried to explain what they had seen and heard to Mudungazi, but Damboia, her eyes flashing, intervened, berating them as no one had done since they had been trained in the use of weapons. And for them, this criticism became all the more impossible to bear coming as it did from the mouth of a woman, a woman of ill fame, even though she belonged to the king's court.

"Is this the elite guard you rely on, Mudungazi? . . . A bunch of cowards, dogs that only know how to bark. What loyalty have you sworn to Muduganzi? What loyalty, you dogs?... No, don't answer me, you've got no right to speak. You should be fed to the vultures. That's what you deserve, you children, you ill-begotten sons! You come here trying to convince us that Mafemane knew of his death and wished to take leave of his wives and children. Why didn't he do it before? Oh, you dogs, imbeciles, idiots, you stupid boys!... Mafemane is preparing to escape, and he's probably already gone. Idiots. And you, Mudungazi, do you still have the courage to give shelter to dogs that only know how to bark? If I were you, I'd kill them... Let's not waste any more time with these idiots. Maguiguane, Mputa, Ualalapi, you go. And take the warriors you want. But don't come back here without Mafemane's body, even if you have to chop down all the forest around you. Get going!"

Ualalapi's wife followed her husband with her gaze until he had disappeared into the forest. She gathered up her son and began to weep gently. She went into her hut and didn't leave until she and her son had died, drowned by their tears that didn't stop flowing from their gaping eyes for eleven days and eleven nights.

Far from his wife's torments, Ualalapi approached Mafemane's village. The sun had turned red. The daylight was ebbing away. When they caught sight of Mafemane's house, Ualalapi and his soldiers stopped some fifteen meters away. Maguiguane and Mputa edged forward to the right and the left, leaving a corridor along the middle at the end of which Mafemane stood waiting for them at the entrance to his house, a smile on his lips.

"I thought you weren't coming," Mafemane said, fixing them with a trenchant, piercing gaze. "You didn't have to bring so many people with you, two would have been enough. But I'm ready. You can kill me. I know you can't go back to your village without my body. I know Mudungazi from childhood. And I know that dissolute wife of his, who goes by the name of Damboia. I don't want to take up your time, you've walked a long way. You can kill me."

Bits of straw floated upwards from a nearby hut. They fluttered in the still air and then fell again. Two birds cut across the sky. A child cried. The mother stifled its weeping. Mafemane smiled. Maguiguane tried to raise his spear. He couldn't. His hand felt leaden. Mputa remained, impassive, without moving. Mafemane smiled. The sun was sinking, crimson. Silence weighed upon them. Night was falling.

From the end of the corridor a spear cut through the air and pierced Mafemane's chest. Tall as he was, his body swayed backwards before returning to its initial position, while he fixed his eyes on the retreating Ualalapi.

"Who is that?" Mafemane asked.

"It's Ualalapi," the warriors nearest him replied.

"Call him. He's got to finish me off, as the laws require. Where's he from?"

"He's Nguni."

"Ah!" He sighed, smiling. His body began to sag. As he bent forward, the spear buried itself more deeply in his blood-soaked chest. With some effort, he reverted to his initial position and coughed up a stream of blood. His knees sank to the ground a few seconds later. He buried his hands in the sand and remained kneeling for a few moments, waiting for Ualalapi, who approached, his head hung. The pain in his chest was such that he fell onto his back, looking up into the sky, where three stars appeared. Lacking the courage to look at him, Ualalapi walked over to Mafemane, knelt down, pulled the spear from his chest, and plunged it back into him again and again. Ualalapi's face, torso and other parts of his body were spattered with the already dead Mafemane's fresh blood. And as the blood ran down Ualalapi's body, he closed his eyes tightly and buried his spear with still greater fury in Mafemane's trunk, which was now riddled with wounds, torn and unrecognisable. Maguiguane and Mputa approached him.

"That's enough," they said, "he's already dead."

Ualalapi stopped his spear just a few centimeters from Mafemane's chest, and got to his feet. He switched his spear to his left hand and started to run through the village screaming "no" in a strident, piercing, hitherto unheard voice. He vanished into the night-shrouded forest, his body crashing through the leaves and branches that his bloodshot eyes could no longer see. Minutes later, the weeping of a woman and a child joined his screams and the forest noises dragged along with them. And the same noise filled the sky and the earth for eleven days and nights, the same number in years ruled by Ngungunyane, the name that Mudungazi adopted when he took power as emperor of all the lands of Gaza.

JEAN SÉNAC

Translated from the French by KAI KRIENKE

Sketch of a Total Body
from *Forebody*

1

The day begins between your teeth,
    barely mumbled, window
Upon the sea. Sun on your lips: the
    beach
Where the poem sprawls.
Here's our summer. I'm only
Transcribing the willowy drone of
    your body.
(I'm thinking of those festivals on
    the barren hills of Bou Saada,
Of those processions in the Spanish

Esquisse d'un Corps Total
de *Avant-Corps*

1

Le jour commence entre tes dents, à
    peine balbutié, fenêtre
Sur la mer. Soleil sur tes lèvres : la
    plage
Où le poème s'étend.
Voici notre été. Je ne fais
Que transcrire le bourdon gracile de
    ton corps.
(Je pense à ces fêtes sur les collines
    arides de Bou Saâda,
À ces processions dans les presqu'îles

Upon his return to Algeria in 1962, shortly after the nation's independence, poet JEAN SÉNAC (1926–1973) famously declared in the "Citizens of Beauty" [Citoyens de beauté]: "And now will we sing love / For there is no Revolution without Love." These lines were not only a declaration of love for the revolution but a call to merge body and politics in Algeria's struggle for independence. His previously repressed homosexuality found a new voice within the emancipation of a people he often called "my people," which he represented through the increasingly erotic "bodypoems" [corpoèmes] he began to write around 1966. Included here are translations of poems written between 1966 and 1970 that became available only posthumously. Sénac's assassination in 1973 can be directly tied to his sexual politics in a nation that was upholding an increasingly conservative definition of its Arab and Muslim heritage.

KAI KRIENKE is a translator, literary reviewer, and Assistant Professor at the Bard High School Early College program in Queens, New York. His work focuses primarily on Algerian poetry in French written during and after the war for independence. He was editor of the Lost & Found series V chapbook on Jean Sénac and is currently translating Sénac's correspondence with Albert Camus.

peninsulas.)

But the day is dawning and I know
That you are there alive
In the curve of my syllables,
The blind man's bluff of my rhythms.
Taking your hand is almost like
    tracing the poem.

Taking your hand is like placing upon
    a carrying rocket
The tools of our consciousness, the
    gems
Of the zodiac, the fantastic colors
    freed
By our passion–hallucinogenic
    health!
(I don't want LSD, I want
Your smile upon the blue of Algiers!)

Grabbing your laughter is like unfold-
    ing the phrases,
Giving them to the wind, with a kiss
Bringing them back to the north
    where in its blue swimsuit
The poem is about to jump upon the

espagnoles.)

Mais le jour commence et je sais
Que là tu es vivante
Dans le galbe de mes syllabes,
Le colin-maillard de mes rythmes.
Prendre ta main c'est presque tracer
    le poème.

Prendre ta main c'est mettre sur leur
    fusée porteuse
Les outils de notre conscience, les
    bijoux
Du zodiaque, les couleurs fantas-
    tiques que libère
Notre passion – santé de
    l'hallucinogène!
(Je ne veux pas de LSD, je veux
Ton rire sur le bleu d'Alger!)

Prendre ton rire c'est déplier les
    phrases,
Les donner au vent, d'un baiser
Les ramener au nord où dans son
    maillot bleu
Le poème s'apprête à sauter sur le

dike.
(In the euphoria of fried foods we
    nearly touch happiness
    with our lips
—Nearly…)

Did we ever know that imagination
Is the insect that punctures the
    poem, our flesh, the horizon,
A destructive chill
    without elytron?
Did we ever know how much rubble
    and horror
Penetrate the blue of the gods, the
    cloud of the sea?
That the waste lingers at the bend of
    an image,
Clogs the heart, and the street
    trembles like murky water,
The voice silts in, the diamond
    is but a stylus.

But you take the word again at its
    wound and you sing,
You open the flame-proof forest
    upon our fires

digue.
(Dans l'euphorie des fritures nous
    touchons presque des
    lèvres le bonheur
—Presque…)

Avons-nous jamais su que
    l'imagination
Est l'insecte qui troue le poème,
    notre chair, l'horizon,
Un froid destructeur sans élytre?
Avons-nous jamais su combien de
    décombres et d'horreurs
Entrent dans le bleu des dieux, dans
    le nuage de la mer?
Que le gâchis s'éternise au détour
    d'une image,
Bouche le cœur, et la rue tremble
    comme une eau trouble,
La voix s'envase, le diamant n'est
    plus qu'un stylet.

Mais tu reprends le mot à sa plaie et
    tu chantes,
Tu ouvres sur nos incendies la forêt
Ignifuge (lentisques au bord de la

(lentisks by the sea).
Nothing is frightening, I write.

2

Thrilling invention, Eros,
When with a single stride you erase
    the beach,
The swimmers turn around,
    amazed,
Until you gush from the foam
    anew,

Poetry, Total Body!

November 29, 1966

mer).
Plus rien n'est redoutable, j'écris.

2

Intervention frémissante, Eros,
Lorsque d'une enjambée tu biffes la
    plage,
Les baigneurs se retournent,
    émerveillés,
Jusqu'à ce qu'à nouveau tu jaillisses
    de l'écume,

Poésie, Corps Total !

29 novembre 1966

The Prince of Aquitaine

from *A-Bodypoem*

The battle until dawn

1

I have made my bed with words.
And the orgasm itself a rocket of
    liquid words.
(In the totality of the body
The charred letter
Of which we only know the secret
    curve
—But toward what urge and with
    what arrow?)

I have made a dwelling with my larva
Between my sheets, and to the end of
The sea (or maybe a tear?)

With my frenetic hiccups
I have made a word to name
The pleasure and the negation
(Upon your lyre my teeth battle the
    ode to the blood).

Le Prince d'Aquitaine

de *A-Corpoème*

L'affrontement jusqu'à l'aube

1

J'ai fait mon lit avec mots.
Et l'orgasme lui-même fusée de mots
    liquides.
(Dans la totalité du corps
La lettre calcinée
Dont nous ne connaissons que la
    courbe secrète
—Mais vers quelle butte ou quelle
    flèche ?)

J'ai fait avec mes larves une hutte
Entre mes draps, et tout au bout
La mer (ou peut-être une larme ?)

J'ai fait avec mes hoquets frénétiques
Un verbe pour nommer
La jouissance et la négation
(Sur ta lyre mes dents affrontent au
    sang l'ode).

I have made my night with your nail
And under your fleece the owl (Sings
Rebellious! Bring to writing
Our uncontrollable saliva!)

With the radiating heat of our
   surprise
(Patiently exalted) – your Cry –
I have made my bed and my poem
(I bury my centuries in your mouth,
   I trace
Upon your walls my fresco – your
   tumors
Howl. I get
Hard. I write
Dizzily suspended
From your nape. O
Insurmountable presence! Lapidated
Space!)

2
You bring back my rust upon your lips.
I drink
Toward the skylight – my kingdom
Was inhabited by prince words.

J'ai fait ma nuit avec ton ongle
Et sous ta toison le hibou (Chante
Rebelle ! Apporte à l'écriture
Notre salive incontrôlée !)

Avec la chaleur irradiée de notre
   surprise
(Patiemment exaltée) – ton Cri –
J'ai fait mon lit et mon poème
(J'enfouis mes siècles dans ta bouche,
   je trace
Sur tes parois ma fresque – tes tumeurs
Hurlent. Je
Bande. J'é-
Cris vertigineusement suspendu
A ta nuque. O
Présence
Insurmontable ! Espace
Lapidé !).

2
Tu ramènes ma rouille sur tes lèvres.
Je bois
Vers la lucarne – mon royaume
Etait peuplé de prince mots.

You bring back the blinding sword
With a tear
And the pedestal where long ago
   Antar tackled the fable.

You bring back the blue of June
And I ransack
The verandas upon your lips
I tear apart underwear I howl
To childhood.

O
Upon your lips bring back
My thistles and the pine
Needle. Reassemble if you can
This body that is going to the dogs.
Give it if you can a password
For this world.

(Slug-words, sting-words!)
If you can, last until dawn with me.

3
File this body

Tu ramènes le glaive aveuglant
D'une larme
Et le socle où jadis Antar
   osa la fable.

Tu ramènes le bleu de Juin
Et je saccage
Sur tes lèvres ces vérandas
Je déchire des slips je hurle
A l'enfance.

O
Sur tes lèvres ramène
Mes chardons et l'aiguille
De pin. Si tu peux
Rassemble ce corps qui fout le camp
   de toutes parts.
Si tu peux donne-lui un mot
De passe pour ce monde.

(Mots-limaces, mots-dards !)
Si tu peux, dure avec moi jusqu'à l'aube.

3
Lime ce corps

Down to the rhyme.
Write your crime with
The Angel's relic.

Cross over
To the other shore (where
Fright
Is but a syllable
Taking refuge on your nape).

This poor body also
Wants its war of liberation!

4
Carry to the Inconsolable
This bone
That he chiseled with his blunders,
This break where my name remains.
(Which sun capsized your tongue?)
Tell him that a cripple awaits him
At the Door of Wandering Words
(Or maybe an astrapia would abolish
    the Tower).

5
Phrases that should allow us

Jusqu'à la rime.
Ecris ton crime avec
Le vestige d'Ange.

Passe
Sur l'autre rive (là
Où l'effroi
N'est sur ta nuque qu'une syllabe
Réfugiée).

Ce pauvre corps aussi
Veut sa guerre de libération !

4
Porte à l'Inconsolé
Cet os
Qu'il a ciselé de ses gaffes,
Cette brisure où dure son nom.
(Quel soleil chavire ta langue ?)
Dis-lui qu'un infirme l'attend
A la porte de Mots Errants
(Peut-être une astrapie abolirait la
    Tour).

5
Phrases qui devraient nous permettre

Vast excursions from one nerve to
    the other, from one bone
To the moon's rock. Phrases
That could only tie us to exile,
To the perishable song, to the tool
Of our chasms. Banal
Seasons upon the most monstrous
    wound.
Jetties to the star.

Ra blues
(To convey a "song of the spheres")

The four houses of
    the world
Have opened for Ra

With rants and trash Afou
Pursues his blind path

But Afou's pain
His tenacious lamentation
    are our pillar.

Afou's stick
Is our stick

De vastes randonnées d'un nerf à
    l'autre, d'un os
Au roc de lune. Phrases
Qui n'avez su que nous amarrer à
    l'exil,
Au chant périssable, à l'outil
De nos gouffres. Saisons
Banales sur la plus monstrueuse plaie.
Jetées à l'astre.

Râ blues
(Pour convoyer un « chant des
    sphères »)

Les quatre maisons du monde
Se sont ouvertes pour Râ

Afou de râles et d'ordures
Poursuit son aveugle parcours

Mais la douleur d'Afou
Sa tenace mélopée sont notre colonne.

Le bâton d'Afou
Est notre bâton

The Fig Tree Laurels

from *derisions and Vertigo/holings*

Come, bitter love.
Through the reeds
Your pink esteem
Is more than a respite.
Maybe a snag, the entry
To the Rip
Beyond which everything
    becomes birth.

✢

I climb onto your hips, Columbus,
    towards fantastic
    countries
Rituals, dances, treasures,
    fantastically luminous and
    naked greet me.
In you I rejoice, in you my austerity
    is a campfire.
Stand up, Aztec column, furnace
    of joy, may

Lauriers du Figuier

Viens, amer.
A travers les roseaux
Ton estime rose
M'est plus qu'un répit.
Peut-être un accroc, l'accès
A la Déchirure
Au-delà de laquelle tout redevient
    naissance.

✢

Je vais sur vos hanches, Colomb, vers
    de fabuleuses
    contrées.
Rites, danses, trésors, fantastiquement
    lumineux et nus
    m'acquiescent.
En toi je me réjouis, en toi mon
    ascèse est un feu de camp.
Erige-toi, colonne aztèque, fournaise
    de joie, que chante

The caravel sing! Battles of pens,
    radiant
Gush, my whole body encloses you.

Cosmonaut!
The seagulls already circle around
    your bathing suit.
Take it off! Here are the Indies! O
My love!
(But in me lies I don't know which
    of Cortez's apprehensions . . .)

Conqueror I surrender to my
    conquest,
Returned to barbaric gods,
Dispossessed.
And I simply become a
    geographer
Towards that cataract where your
    innocence leads,
The enraptured explorer of the
    river and the flora,
Celebrating in this beverage I know
    not what funeral rite.

La caravelle ! Batilles de plumes, jets
Radieux, tout mon corps sur toi se
    referme.

Cosmonaute !
Sur ton slip déjà tournoient
    les mouettes.
Retire-le ! Voici les Indes ! O
Mon amour !
(Mais en moi demeure je ne sais
    quelle appréhension de Cortez…)

Conquérant me voici soumis par ma
    conquête,
Rendu aux dieux barbares,
Dépossédé.
Et je deviens tout simplement le
    géographe
Vers cette cataracte où ton innocence
    m'entraîne,
L'explorateur émerveillé du fleuve et
    de la flore,
Célébrant en cette libation je ne sais
    déjà quel rite funèbre.

✤

I suck you and you cry : "Give me
    joy!"
As though I didn't know from what
    abyss that oil came.

✤

I thought I had only two arms, two
    legs, one sex,
You make me find the milky dragon
With a thousand limbs, the arabesques
    of my senses.
Another word whose first utterance
    is a groan.
Savage syllables and savage body.
And having given me America you
    return to your temples.

✤

You are my perpetual presence.
You shouldn't have given me access
    to pleasure.

✤

Je te suce et tu cries : « Réjouis-
    moi ! »
Comme si je ne sais de quel abîme il
    fallait tirer ce pétrole.

✤

Je croyais n'avoir que deux bras, deux
    jambes, un sexe,
Tu me fais retrouver le dragon lacté,
Aux mille membres, les arabesques
    de mes sens.
Une autre parole dont le gémisse-
    ment est l'inflexion première.
Syllabes sauvages et corps sauvage.
Et m'ayant donné l'Amérique tu te
    retires dans tes temples.

✤

Tu es la perpétuelle présence.
Il ne fallait pas me donner accès au
    plaisir.

Memory, imagination – and my hand!
You stay with me!

(And there we redraw the course of
    rivers, the shape of trees, the
    sumptuous beasts.
Under my fingers we are reborn in
    such perfect unity
That the column crumbles – and with
    a cry I touch death.)

✧

Your lyre and your fleece,
Your teeth where I canoe,
Your thighs where the future is written
    in harrowing games.
The simulation of the tempest, the
    tempest, forgetting the tempest.
Hardly a word, idiot, to announce
    pleasure and death, thank you.
And your pupils returning to their
    planets
You leave me alone with my anxious
    joy – the impact of flying saucers.

Mémoire, imagination – et la main !
Avec moi tu restes !

(Et là nous refaisons le cours des
    fleuves, la
Forme des arbres, les bêtes
Fastueuses.
Sous mes doits nous renaissons dans
    une unité si parfaite
Que la colonne s'écroule – et d'un cri
    je touche à la mort.)

✧

Ta lyre et ta toison,
Tes dents où je pirogue,
Tes cuisses où l'avenir s'écrit en jeux
    poignants.
La simulation de la tempête, la
    tempête, l'oubli de la tempête
Un mot à peine, idiot, pour annoncer
    plaisir et mort, merci.
Et tes pupilles qui regagnent leur
    planète.
Tu me laisses seul avec mon angoissante
    joie – l'impact

(Returning to the laboratories.
Recomposing your lyre and your
    fleece.
The only palpable thing I have is
    writing.
Triumphant failure, bodypoem!)

✛

Your saliva your sperm,
That body you have embellished
    with your traces,
Your sweat, my crazy zodiac,
Perishable legend, of that Tassili
Will only my words be left?

✛

O my thousands of adolescents
I'll be familiar with you, can I?
From Morgeat or from Tamadecht,
From Paris or from Barcelona.
From Bad-el-Oued or from Moscow
(And you my St. James's pilgrims
    where Nerval inhales the
Darkness on your knees).

des soucoupes volantes.

(Retourner aux laboratoires.
Recomposer ta lyre et ta toison.
Je n'ai d'écriture que palpable.
Corpoème, échec triomphant !)

✛

Ta salive et ton sperme,
Ce corps que tu as embelli de tes
    traces,
Ta sueur, mon zodiaque fou,
Légende périssable, de ce Tassili
Ne restera-t-il que mes mots ?

✛

O mes milliers d'adolescents
Je te tutoie veux-tu ?
De Morgeat ou de Tamadecht,
De Paris ou de Barcelone.
De Bab-el-Oued ou de Moscou
(Et vous mes pèlerins de Saint-
    Jacques où Nerval aspire
La ténèbres sur vos genoux).

Being familiar with you because
    you are.
In the futile lightning of your teeth
    and thighs
No dragon of my delights
But the only dove and my only virtue.

(And you my vacationers, donors
    under tents
Of the first name of every wave,
Of the sun of each wound,
Maybe in the delirium of the Fig Tree
    Another Beauty has begun
        its journey?)

✧

Bitter love,
But at least your leaves are not sharp,
And the adolescents on the beach
    wear bathing suits with your colors.
When the reeds shiver
Your pink mixes its
Insolence and modesty with our ink.
Here,
Today again,

Te tutoie car tu es.
Dans le futile éclair de tes dents et
    des cuisses
Non le dragon de mes délices
Mais l'unique colombe et ma seule
    vertu.

(Et vous mes estivants, donateurs
    sous les tentes
Du prénom de chaque vague,
Du soleil de chaque plaie,
Peut-être dans ces délires du
    Figuier une Autre Beauté
s'est-elle mise en route ?)

✧

Amer,
Mais du moins tes feuilles ne sont
    pas coupantes.
Et les adolescents sur la plage
    portent des maillots à tes couleurs.
Quand les roseaux frémissent
Ton rose vient mêler à notre encre
Son insolence et sa pudeur.
Ici,

Under jeers and laws,
Assailed lamp and sun,
In poverty, projection, space,
Under your vigil,
I reign.

Le Figuier, August 10–11, 1970

Aujourd'hui encore,
Sous les quolibets et les lois,
Quinquet assailli et soleil,
Dans la pauvreté, la saillie, l'espace,
Sous ta vigie,
Je règne.

Le Figuier, 10-11 août 1970

EMMANUEL DONGALA

Translated by SARA C. HANABURGH

Group Photo
by the Riverside

EMMANUEL BOUND-ZEKI DONGALA, born in 1941 in Congo-Brazzaville, is an award-winning writer whose formal educational training in the Sciences led him to spend a good portion of his life working as a chemistry professor while he simultaneously directed the Théâtre de l'Éclair and was President of the National Association of Congolese Writers in Brazzaville. The civil war forced the writer/scientist and his family to seek refuge elsewhere. When France outright denied him asylum, he was welcomed by friends he had made in literary circles in the U.S., and in 1998 was invited to join the faculty at Bard College at Simon's Rock, where he taught chemistry and French and Francophone literature. Dongala is best known for his child soldier narrative, *Johnny Chien Méchant* (2002), translated into English as *Johnny Mad Dog* in 2005 and adapted for the screen in 2008. But his literary oeuvre, comprised of five novels, one short story collection and two plays, is much more vast and diverse in theme and style.

IT IS EASIER to get into heaven than into the private apartments of the President of the Republic and the First Lady.

The first roadblock was at the tall gate that opened into the courtyard of the complex. The two soldiers guarding the roadblock asked where you were going and if you had a mission order or a summons. The driver explained. A call made to you-don't-know-who confirmed that they were indeed waiting for you, just you, not the driver, he was asked to turn around. So you had to cover the last few meters on foot. As you watched the guards, you had the vivid recollection of the day Iyissou's son had been arrested. He was coming back from a refugee camp when he was struck down, loaded into a truck and taken to an undisclosed destination. What if these soldiers had been part of the sinister commando that had raided the loading docks of the city's river port that day?

You advanced toward the second roadblock, which was more sophisticated with a security office, armed soldiers, and two tanks with their canons pointed toward the avenue that led to the high wall surrounding the buildings and the entrance gate. You noticed the video cameras that were no doubt recording your every movement.

A woman soldier frisked you, patted you down to make sure you weren't hiding a bomb in your panties. She confiscated your cell phone, your bag of madeleines, too, then waved you through. Apparently, you were no longer a danger to the Republic. Finally, you penetrated the inner walls of the President and First Lady's private residence.

First, the space. Coming, as you did, from a working-class neighborhood where vital air occupied a mere few square meters and where several people shared a small room and sometimes the same bed, one could barely fathom having so much space for oneself alone. You admired the mown green lawn, the sprinkler spraying, its arms swiveling with each spurt of hydraulic pressure. Palm trees including several ravenalas, traveller's palms, with fanned leaves marked precise paths around the grounds. Two magnificent peacocks strutted about on the lawn, one fanning its beautiful tail spotted with specks of bluish sheen. A little farther on, you could see deckchairs under umbrellas. And the pool, of course.

You were staring in amazement at this verdant paradise when a guard called out to you and signaled for you to follow him to the waiting room. You passed by a garage and counted one Aston Martin, two Japanese SUVs and an empty spot. A Rolls-Royce perhaps? You let your imagination run wild for a split second: you had never sat in a Rolls. Maybe, like the Minister, the First Lady would have you driven back in hers or in one of the luxury SUVs?

The guard escorted you into the sitting room and asked you to take a seat and wait your turn. You looked around. My God! You wondered if you could place your buttocks down on one of those luxurious leather armchairs or feel modestly content on one of the benches. You figured you'd opt for the luxury armchair since your buttocks were worth just as much as the country's first lady's, right? The seat felt soft, you placed your arms on the armrests and you settled comfortably into the chair. It truly was better than that armchair at the Ministry of Women and Disabled Persons with its springs that poked through the back of the chair and kept you from nestling in. But you were not the only one in the room. Three other well-dressed women were waiting too, two squeezed on the sofa, the other, younger and alone, sat stiffly on one of the benches. They all outright ignored you, perhaps they took you for a rival who'd come to beg for help from the woman the national radio called the "Mother of the Nation." They continued to ostensibly watch the television or, rather, the televisions because there were five—two with giant screens—each tuned to a different channel. On the French-language channel, people were playing Questions for a Champion. One of the English channels was showing American Idol, the other, CNN, an American 24-hour news channel, streamed more advertisements than news, and then there was the Arabic channel Al-Jazeera. The last TV tuned to a local channel had just shown some traditional dances and was re-airing the speech the Head of State had given the previous evening.

Seated comfortably in your cushy chair, you looked up at the ceiling. Although you were no expert in architecture, you were sure that those delicately molded geometric structures must have cost a fortune; you wondered if the faux rustic columns standing in the four corners of the room were made of real marble. At the end of the room there was a bar and several bottles of wine and liquor

Group Photo By the Riverside (*Photo de Groupe au bord du fleuve*, Actes Sud, 2010) narrates the story of Méréana Rangi, an ordinary woman who is left penniless after divorcing from her power-hungry corrupt husband, Tito Rangi. She takes a job at a quarry breaking stones into gravel and despite herself, becomes the spokesperson for her entire cohort of fifteen women when they demand to be paid a fairer price for their labor. The passage excerpted here picks up from about halfway through the novel, as Méréana arrives for her meeting with the First Lady at the presidential residence to defend her group's protest, in spite of rumors that those who have been summoned to penetrate the palace gates disappear forever into its torture chambers concealed in the basement.

lined up behind the counter. The space must also be used for receptions, you thought. Maybe, even, if you turned on the faucet you noticed over on the counter, champagne would flow instead of water because in those circles, it seemed to be the drink of choice. Your head began to spin. Never before had you seen such luxury, never would you have imagined that in this country all you had to do was go through a gate to find yourself on the other side of the mirror, in a world where poverty and misery did not exist and where one did not have to break stone in order to survive. A world where one likely didn't die because how could death reach you when you lived in the middle of such insolent luxury?

After waiting several minutes, you were called ahead of the women who were there before you into an office or rather a living room and there you were finally face to face with Madam First Lady. You had only seen her through televised news programs when she made donations in the name of her organization, Childhood-Solidarity, which she described as non-governmental, even though everyone knew it received three quarters of its funding from State money. In the flesh, unlike the Minister, she was wearing African dress, which played to her advantage, a three-piece ensemble, the pagne and head wrap made from the same fabric. It made her look dignified as a leader's wife should look and at the same time gave her a reassuring maternal look. A little toward the back was a woman with a notebook, probably her secretary. No doubt about it, you were impressed. Without getting up, she said:

"You are Méréana Rangi?"

"Yes, Madam."

"Hello."

"Hello."

"Sit down."

You sat down, stiff, petrified almost. It was still difficult for you to realize that you were sitting there, face to face with the country's first lady, in her residence. And yet, although the minister had warned you that the president's wife was very upset with you, the few sentences she'd spoken up to that point did not ring of anger.

"You are young. You could be my daughter, you know. You look nothing like the fury you've been described as."

"…"

"So, you're rallying women against me?"

She struck you with those words suddenly without warning. You felt intimidated, you didn't know how to react, or even what to say.

"Uh… uh…"

"Uh what? You know, I know everything."

"I think there's some misunderstanding, Madam First Lady, we're not rallying anyone against you, we're just women asking for a better price for our bags of stones."

"It seems you threw stones at the police. Is that reasonable?"

"We were under attack by gunfire."

"One of you is in a coma?"

"Yes, madam."

"It's sad all of that. So you see where it leads when one does not follow the appropriate channels to make protests? You've heard of the NGO Childhood-Solidarity, haven't you?"

"Yes, Madam."

"And do you know who runs it?"

"Yes. You do."

SARA HANABURGH is a scholar of African literatures and cinemas, co-translator of Boubacar Boris Diop's *Kaveena* and translator of Angèle Rawiri's *The Fury and Cries of Women*. Her articles and translations have appeared in *Nouvelles Études Francophones*, *The Dictionary of African Biography* and *Warscapes*.

"So then, why didn't you come to see me to discuss your issues? Don't you know that that NGO also deals with women's issues?"

"Because… because… demanding a better price for one's merchandise is not a women's issue."

"What bizarre reasoning. Are you a woman or not?"

"Yes, but not in this case."

She looks at you oddly.

"Excuse me? Sometimes you're a woman, sometimes you're not?"

"Uh… no… I'm talking about women's demands."

You were definitely doing a poor job of explaining yourself because she clearly still didn't understand and interrupted you, tactfully not suggesting that something was out of whack in your brain.

"Listen," she went on, "there's going to be a big women's celebration in our country. It will not just be a first ladies' event because as Mother of the Nation, I want all the women in our country to participate. There is no issue you could have that I cannot resolve."

"Our bags of stones…"

"I know. You want to sell them for twenty thousand francs, you want someone to return to you the bags that were confiscated by the police because you refused to obey and attacked the policemen. I know all of that. All of that will be taken care of; but, as that may take some time, I'm going to ask you one thing: cease your protests immediately and any demonstrations while the matter is being resolved. I do not want any unrest or any perception of unrest hanging over the country while my guests are here. I know you are a reasonable young woman, and that you would not want this conference or this country to fall apart. Nor would you want the President to be shamed in front of the rest of the world."

"It will be difficult for us to stop our protests because…"

"Listen, my child – I can call you my child because I am as old as your mother – you are their spokesperson; I've been told how well you speak, how at a meeting in the hospital courtyard you kept those women from marching on the police station. That's what I appreciate about you, the intelligent way you have of seeing a situation in front of you and the courage to change opinions about it. That's why, in spite of my very busy schedule at the moment, I took the time to meet with you and, better yet, I had you in before all those women you saw in the waiting room and who have been waiting for hours to be seen. That can only prove to you the high regard I have for you. I know those women will listen to you if you tell them to stop your protests while I address your matter and I give you my word that I will do that. Tito Rangi is a deputy now, and that's thanks to me. Better yet, he is an advisor to the president thanks to my intervention."

The mention of Tito's name irritates you.

"Tito has nothing to do with this."

"It's to make you understand that what I did for him, I can also do for you. You think I don't know anything about you? Your sister for example. We never met, but I respected her because she was a woman who honored our nation. Be responsible like she was. Ask the women to stop their protests. If they do, I will personally see to it that the matter is settled – I've already made it my business anyway. How do you think your comrades got released so easily after committing aggravated assault against the police?"

She stopped speaking and looked at you, which meant she was waiting for an answer.

"Because of your intervention."

"Exactly! I'll say it again, this meeting with the first ladies, this big celebration of our country, is too important to me."

She stopped again and looked at you. You said nothing, not because you didn't know what to say, but because you were trying to figure out how to formulate a way you could articulate to the First Lady, the Mother of the Nation, your outright refusal to betray your friends, by renouncing what had already cost you so dearly. Remind her that one of you was in a coma? Seeing that you were not taking the bait in spite of all the compliments she had showered you with, she said sharply:

"I know that you need a hundred twenty thousand francs."

With that, you panicked a little. How did she know that? What else did she know about you? She persisted:

"A hundred twenty thousand francs is no problem. I am very sensitive to women's suffering and it's that sensitivity that can at times pass for maternalism. Helping women get by, gain their independence from men, helping them take their destinies into their own hands, it's what I live for, otherwise what would be the use of being the First Lady? And of being a mother? You may not know it but I am also a mother.

"I fight poverty by going onto the battleground, into villages where I distribute palm oil to women, medicine, powdered milk for their babies, mills to grind foufou and tables and benches for schools. Once I even took responsibility for the hospital bill of a woman who had given birth to quintuplets! Better yet, I insisted to my husband that the number of women in the next Parliament must double. We will thus move from fifteen percent of women today to thirty percent, a major step toward complete equality in a very near future. And then there's my program to fight HIV/AIDS. Heeding the advice of the Churches, I've just added abstinence and reintegration of prostitutes because the fewer of those there are, the fewer people with and at risk of contracting AIDS there will be. Know that this fight I am leading against AIDS and for development is cited as an example throughout the whole world. The choice of our country to house this important meeting is not by chance, but rather a consecration, recognition of the work that I do. Do you see how important it is now? I am going to take care of your personal problem right away. For the rest of your demands, they will be dealt with immediately following the conference. I give you my word."

She turned to the woman you believed to be her secretary who took a thick manila envelope out of a drawer and handed it to Madam. The latter placed it down conspicuously on her desk.

"There is well more than you need to get by in this envelope. For your studies, for your future. It's yours."

You were absolutely stunned! You had heard about corruption, you knew it was rampant in the country, but you had never confronted it. Up to that moment there was absolutely no doubt in your mind that you were incorruptible. But right there in front of you was that envelope. All you would have to do was extend your hand, take it, put it in your purse, no questions asked and all your problems would be solved. By the following day, you'd be able to pay the fees for your computer courses and in six months you could maybe open your own school, your own business, and just like that realize the broken dream of your youth. And you would no longer deny your children the simple pleasures one is entitled to at that age. In any case, in life, one must know how to seize an opportunity and often that opportunity, unlike the mailman, rarely rings twice at your door. And after all, she had stolen that money from the state's coffers, right? That meant it belonged to you a little as well. So, why not reap the benefits of it?

With her experience in corrupting people, the lady had become adept at reading facial movements and could immediately detect who could be bought off right then and there and who would hesitate and need a little push to get over their wavering reluctance. She must have considered you in the second category since, after she'd observed you for a moment, she continued in a soft voice, intended to sound reassuring:

"What happens in this office stays in this office. No one will ever know anything. Here, take it."

For the first time since you'd been in there, she stood up. Standing in front of you in her expensive outfit, her presence was even more intimidating. You looked up at her. She walked toward you, the envelope in her hand. She held it out to you. You looked at the object, a fat manila envelope. It was sealed. You did not move an inch. She watched you for a moment then tapped on your shoulder three or four times and said in a motherly tone: "Go ahead, take it, it's nothing, it's just to help you." You contemplated the object again for a few seconds then suddenly you grabbed it and shoved it in your purse. The transaction was complete. You got up. Then, the great compassionate lady, modestly triumphant, wrapped an arm around your shoulders and said with a knowing smile:

"Don't make it more of an issue than is necessary, my child. And don't worry, you are not the first person to be reasonable and choose where your priorities lie. In about two hours, a television crew will be advised about your meeting where you will release a press statement announcing that you have decided to cease your protests until the end of the First Ladies of Africa meeting. It will not be a betrayal. In fact, to the contrary, the President of the Republic will consider your decision a patriotic gesture toward the nation. Good luck. I'm counting on you."

She turned away from you and returned to her armchair. Her problem solved, she had already forgotten you. Her secretary escorted you out. If she had been a man, you would have considered her a "henchman" of the First Lady of the Republic. Can we also say "henchwoman"? Your mind did not register anything on your inverse path out of the presidential residence. Only when the humid warmth suddenly assaulted you did you realize that you'd already exited the air-conditioned buildings. At the security office, you were handed your cell phone but not your bag of madeleines. You asked for them. Threatening, the guard replied that all you had left was your cell phone, nothing else. My god, military personnel who swipe madeleines, you thought. You didn't insist. You took the phone and you put it in your bag on top of that manila envelope that was worth its weight in thirty pieces of silver.

Hassan Hajjaj,
Wamuhu, 2015

BREYTEN BREYTENBACH

"that ship has flown"

(a Nigerian remembering
    Pan-Africanism)

in the small hours when moon
already behind a veil of waxing
    absence
lowers her dark body weightlessly
into the pool of darkness,
and I in quiet conversation
with a poem

about thisses and thats and death

"that ship has flown"

(a Nigerian remembering
    Pan-Africanism)

laatnag toe die maan reeds
agter 'n sluier van toenemende afwe-
    sigheid
haar donker lyf in die kuil
van donkerte gewigloos laat sink,
en ek in rustige gesprek
met 'n gedig

oor ditte en datte en die dood

An outspoken human rights activist, **BREYTEN BREYTENBACH** is a poet, painter, memoirist, essayist, and novelist. His paintings and drawings have been exhibited around the world. Born in South Africa, he emigrated to Paris in the late '60s and became deeply involved in the anti-Apartheid movement. Author of *Mouroir, A Season in Paradise, The True Confessions of an Albino Terrorist, Dog Heart, The Memory of Birds in Times of Revolution, A Veil of Footsteps*, among many others, Breytenbach received the Alan Paton Award for *Return to Paradise* in 1994 and the prestigious Hertzog Prize for Poetry for *Papierblom* in 1999 and for *Die Windvanger* (*Windcatcher*) in 2008.

that has to be seen to,
stillness which must be shared
(so little time and so much
    still to do, tomorrow),

someone or something thumps
    against the pane.

a messenger? a night-wanderer
who lost the way?
a friend with the thwack of a soggy
newspaper urgently bringing tidings
of injured nightingales?
or a blind drunk angel?

I shush my finger to the poem's lips,
go to the window
with its dim reflection,
look down at the late night garden
shrouded in silence
where stones will smoulder
    tomorrow:

nothing.

waarna omgesien moet word,
stilte wat gedeel moet word
(so min tyd en so veel
    nog te doen, môre),

bons iets of iemand teen die ruit.

'n boodskapper? 'n nagswerwer
wat die pad byster geraak het?
'n vriend wat met 'n nat koerant
se floerps dringend nuus wil bring
van beseerde nagtegale?
of 'n blindedronk engel?

ek lê my vinger op die gedig se lippe,
loop na die venster
met my dowwe weerkaatsing,
kyk uit en af op die laatnag tuin
gehul in stilte
waar klippe môre sal smeul:

niks.

and when I turn back the workroom
   is empty,
no face in the dead glass,
no poem.

it was Plato who recalled
that the pucker of gooseflesh on the
   nape
     and fore-arms
is a shivered reminder
where feathers used to grow

(from "The Singing Hand,"
   unpublished)

en met die omdraai is die werkka-
mer leeg,
geen gesig in die dooie glas,
geen gedig.

dis Plato wat onthou het
die pluksels hoendervleisvel in die
nek
     en op voorarms
is waar vere vantevore gegroei het
     se rilling geheue

measures

you can't let a drunken man hold a
   pen
he will try to tack and sail against
   history

you can't let a drunken man leave the

maatreëls

jy kan nie 'n dronk man 'n pen vas
   laat hou
hy sal aanhou probeer om teen
   geskiedenis te laveer

jy kan nie 'n dronk man voordag die

house
before dawn
when streetlights are still green
he will go to the quay to bellow at
the wind

you can't ask a drunken man to think
straight
he will tell you all about rodents in
Siberia

you can't let a drunken man walk
through town
where sloe-eyed women have long
and sly looks
he will stumble over his words and
his feet
and go piss behind the laurel bush in
the park
with a shiver down his spine

truly, you can't ask a drunken man
how about a poem
he will pull faces by the window at
passers-by

huis uit laat gaan
wanneer straatligte nog groen
is nie
hy sal op die kaai teen die wind staan
en bulk

jy kan nie 'n dronk man vra om
reguit te dink nie
hy sal vir jou vertel van knaagdiere in
Siberië

jy kan nie 'n dronk man in die dorp
laat loop
waar vrouens lang oë soos
slange het nie
hy sal struikel oor sy voete en sy
woorde
en agter die lourierbos in die park
met 'n rilling al langs sy rug af
gaan pis

jy kan mos nie 'n dronk man vra wat
is 'n gedig nie
hy sal by die venster gesigte trek vir
verbygangers

and pretend he's looking to rhyme
    with luck

you can't believe a drunken man
    when he says he has flown
even if he's covered in bumps and
    bruises
and though a dirty pair of under-
    pants
be slapping the flagpole on city hall

you cannot ask a drunken man after
    the whereabouts of God
he will intimate that his underpants
    have been stolen

you can't allow a drunken man to
    work on the roof
he will tell you he knows the ins and
    outs of the sound of singing
while in his naked skin listening to
    the greediest secrets
whispered in chimney flues

en vir jou sê hy soek 'n rymwoord vir
    knak

jy kan nie vir 'n dronk man glo
    as hy sê hy het gevlieg nie
al is hy vol knoppe en
    kneusplekke
en al wapper daar ook 'n vuil onder-
    broek
aan die vlagpaal bo die stadsaal

jy kan nie vir 'n dronk man vra waar
    is God nie
hy sal vir jou sê sy onderbroek is
    gesteel

jy kan nie 'n dronk man op die dak
    laat werk nie
hy sal vir jou sê hy weet alles van die
    katafoniek
terwyl hy kaalgat die mees afgunstige
    geheime
by die skoorsteen af luister en
    fluister

you can't question him at all about love
for as a drunken suitor he will stumble
when he offers you his heart in a bag
        of rotten tomatoes
            while his mouth is still red

you can't expect a drunken man
        to snitch on dead friends
he has a knife with a white blade in
        his pocket

you can't inquire of a drunken man
        if he ever thinks of death
he splutters too much when he
        curses and laughs

verily, I say to you
you can't have a drunken man
cry on paper
    it becomes a shitting of flies
        with tears and snot
        and old wine stains
            here

(from "The Singing Hand,"
unpublished)

jy kan hom nie uitvra oor die liefde
    nie
want as dronk vryer sal hy steier
en vir jou sy hart aanbied soos 'n
        kardoes vrot tamaties
            terwyl sy mond nog rooi is

jy kan nie dat 'n dronk man jou vertel
        van sy dooie vriende nie
hy het 'n langlem-mes in sy sak

jy kan nie by 'n dronk man wil weet
        wat hy dink van die dood nie
hy proes te veel wanneer hy die
        brood probeer eet
jy kan nie vir 'n dronk man laat huil
        op papier
dit word 'n vlieëstrontery tussen
        trane en snot
            en ou vlekke wyn
                hier

the dance of the stones

my friend says: this world is so
    resonant
nobody can complete it with
    understanding
but in the beginning it was empty
except for these stones
like clotted thoughts where darkness
    rings

my friend says this is what happens
to the petrified shadowing of stars
    and this is what happens
when you look down the well to
    reveal
the one appearance in the shine of
    the other—
does the heart not remember?

for how will you bring presence in
    the poem?

my friend says: death and poetry –

die dans van die klippe

my vriend sê: dis so 'n groot wêreld
niemand kan dit vol maak met begrip nie
maar aan die begin was dit leeg
behalwe vir die klippe
wat klonte gedagtes van die buitenste
    roepruim is.

my vriend sê dit is wat gebeur
met die versteende skaduwees van sterre
en dit is wat gebeur wanneer jy af in die
    purper put
die een verskynsel in die skyn van die ander
    wil lees

want hoe neem jy teenwoordigheid in die
    gedig?

my vriend vra: die dood en die digkuns –
is dit nie één nie? en die voël en die wind –
kan die een sonder die ander se vlug
    bestaan?

are these not the same? and bird and
    wind –
can the one fly without the other?
and when light is born in that
    repetition
between shredding of night-stars
and day's invisibility
from the colour of movement?

is this not but a description of
    hovering words?

then my friend says: to pick up
    imagination like stones
and hand them out as bread to the
    hungry
is movement
and to move is to reach out to
    rhythm
for this is the dance
        dance
          dance
this is the pas-de-deux of tolerance
this the whispered wordhouse of
    generosity

en wanneer die lig wat ontklee word
tussen die verflentering van
    nagsterre
en die onsigbaarheid van dag
die kleur van wind is?

maar ook dit slegs 'n beskrywing van
    swewende skrywe?

toe sê my vriend: om verbeelding
op te tel soos klippe en uit te deel
    aan die broodnodiges
is 'n beweging
en om te beweeg is die uitreik na
    ritme
dit is die dans
        dans
          dans
dansende pas-de-deux van ver-
    draagsaamheid
dis die gefluisterde woordhuis van
    vrygewigheid
wanneer jy slegs die ek het om weg
    te gee
en vergewe. kyk, die vryheid

when you have but the I to give
and forgive. look, freedom
of weigh-and-deliver moves hither
    and forth
between contract-relax-contract of
    attachment
and the pendulum cringing of the
    bird-throbbing heart:

look again – the naked madman who
    walked the streets of Luanda
for three long years carrying his
    innards
as carrion in the bowl of his hands
was a dancing reporter of life

here then the pattern: emptiness is
    form
in the beginning, and to make it
    shiver
you have to perfect birds as word-
    shadows,
to sliver and flit words as the shadows
    of birds

van weeg-en-weggee beweeg heen en
    weer
tussen die spanning en ontspanning
    van verbintenis
en die ritmiese saamkrimp van die
    klopvoëlhart:
kyk nog 'n keer – die naakte malman
    wat drie jaar lank
deur die strate van Luanda geloop
    het
met sy derms gedra in die bakkie van
    sy hande
was 'n dansende opskrywer van die
    lewe

dit is die patroon: leegheid is vorm
aan die begin, en om dit te laat bewe
moet jy dit vol maak met die voëls-
    kaduwees van woorde

want aan die een kant en dan weer
    aan die ander.
want hoe neem jy anders die wind se
    woorde in die gesig?

for on the one hand and then on the
    other –
how else will you take wind's worth
    in the face?

(from "The Singing Hand,"
    unpublished)

the to-end

then Wordpig brought the woman
    and the child
to the dark city stinking of death
where blood on the sidewalks is a
    silver skin.

don't look the word-glutton said
for there is nothing to see
except weeping people tearing their
    garments

for death is nothing. death says

die na-einde

toe bring Woordvark die vrou en die
    kind
na die donker stad wat stink na dood.
waar bloed op die sypaadjies 'n silwer
    huid is.

moenie kyk nie sê die woordvraat toe.
daar is niks om te sien
behalwe wenende mense wat hulle
    bo-klede skeur

want die dood is niks. die dood sê

nothing.
and where shall we turn to
where there's no evil?

in many regions searching for truth
    is now
to blindly jab a stick in the soil
and know with the reek of
    putrefaction:

death is here. here too
a trail of raw remembrances on the
    tarmac.
and yet it was life.

it is ours we lug it along
the world is in our dream
and in our stare

to not look away.
don't look. death
designs nothing. death signals

nothing. look the dead only cling
to the living's thoughts

niks.
en waarheen sal ons ons tog wend
waar daar nié onheil is nie?

in baie lande is die sekerheidsoeke
    nou
om blind 'n stok in die aarde te stamp
en met die walm van ontbinding-
    stank

te weet. hier is dood. ook hiér
'n sleepsel rou aandenkings op die
    asfalt.
en tog was dit die lewe.

dis *ons* s'n ons dra dit saam
die wêreld is in ons
droom en in ons kyk

om nie weg te kan kyk nie.
moenie kyk nie. die dood
teken niks. die dood beduie

niks. kyk die dooies kleef maar net
aan die lewendes se verlore gedagtes

in poems and dreams tearing upper
    garments.

then Wordhog told the woman and
    the child
the moon which I wound up so often
is a metaphor for death's silver hide

when dead-winged sailors wash up
in the night of forgetting and
    ascension's
rise and decay to sheeted

darkness. it's the word I looked for
Wordpig says to the woman and the
    child:
sheet to cover the dead

with the faces of the living.
if only for a moment lasting forever
in the city where dark ink

is poured to spell out and pair
light and blood silvering the street:

in gedigte en drome wat die bo-klede
    skeur.

toe sê Woordvark vir die vrou en die
    kind
die maan wat ek so baie verstel het
is 'n metafoor vir sterwe se silwer huid

wanneer dooievlerk matrose uitspoel
in die nag van vergeet en opgaan
se kom en vergaan tot duisternis

gelaken. dis die woord wat ek gesoek
    het
sê Woordvark vir die vrou en die kind:
laken om die dooies toe te maak

met die lewendes se gesigte.
al is dit net vir 'n oomblik wat ewig
    duur
in die stad waar donker ink

geskink word om op straat
in lig en bloed silwerig te paar en spel:

tu caca es mi caca.
your house is my home
and your death which is mine tells
  nothing
of journeys that cannot be measured

to disappearance which cannot be
  known.
you must feast on the words.
you must not know how endless

dying is. for death is nothing.
let me forget and go up in the
  darkness
of coming to go

Wordpig says to the woman and the
  child.
it is but a moment
lasting forever.

don't look

tu caca es mi caca.
julle huis is my tuiste
en julle dood wat my dood is vertel niks
van reise wat nie gemeet kan word nie

na verdwyning wat nie geweet kan
  word nie.
julle moet verder vreet aan die woorde.
julle moenie weet hoe eindeloos

is sterwe nie. want die dood
  is niks.
laat my vergeet en opgaan in kom
en vergaan se duisternis

sê Woordvark vir die vrou en die
  kind.
dis tog net 'n oomblik
wat vir ewig duur.

moenie kyk nie

the to-death

four in the morning
restless sleep filled with dreams
of journeys that cannot
              be measured
of journeys that cannot
              be known
a house creaks
like the joints of eternity
rooms so heavy
with the heady smell
of sweet rotting guavas
bananas avocadoes pineapple
the fruits of a life

know of astral bodies
              still flaming in the night
before the veil of light
              erases them
know the mountain is a sombre lump
filled with pent-up noises of gnashing
    life
              in the earth

die na-dood

vieruur in die môre
onrustige slaap vol drome
van reise na wat nie
gemeet kan word nie
van reise wat nie geweet
              kan word nie
'n huis se kraak
soos die litte van ewigheid
vertrekke so swaar
met die bedwelmende reuk
van soet verrottende koejawels
piesangs avokadopere pynappel
die vrugte van 'n lewe

weet van ruimteliggame
              wat nog vlam in die nag
voor die sluier van lig
              hulle uit sal vee
weet die berg is 'n donker homp
vol ingehoue geluide van knarsende
    lewe
              in die grond

know the mountain will yet spit stars
in patterns of journeys
          that cannot be measured

know the sea will always be there
          in the night
a black flag flapping over
    dreams
know too that no knowing
          can ever say the sea

and know that one is human
among wandering humans
each with the fire of dying

and know one's people came
          to go
that love was made
laughed and wept
and each laid down a dream
like a stone bannered in a landscape
          of nights
which must spell out the journey
          that cannot be told
in the dark light that cannot
          be measured

---

weet die berg sal nog steeds sterre
          spoeg
in patrone van reise wat nie gemeet
          kan word nie

weet die see sal altyd daar wees
          in die nag
'n donker wappervlag oor drome
weet ook dat geen verstand die see
          ooit kan beskryf nie

en weet dat jy mens is
tussen dolende mense
elk met die vuur van sterwe

en weet jou mense het gekom
om te gaan
dat daar liefde gemaak is
gelag en geween
en elkeen 'n droom neergelê het
soos 'n steen gevaandel in 'n landskap
          van nagte
die reis wat nie geweet kan word nie
          uit moet spel
in die duister lig wat nie
          gemeet kan word nie

until here: you and yours and we
and I too
the daybreak dusk
a silence before the song of birds

with these verses faintly sketched
in the void's glow
love jingles   ritournelles
                for the sorrow
rallying calls for resistance
                of the dead
light that's long since gone
to flare only now
scars   muttered tales
of journeys that cannot be measured
to disappearance that cannot be
    known

Sea Point, October 2015

tot hier: jy en joune en ons
en ook ek
die dagskemering
'n stilte voor die sang van voëls

met hierdie verse vaag geteken
in niet se skynsel:
liefdesrympies   opsêgoed
                vir die verdriet
roepkrete tot die dooies
            se verset
lig wat lankal weg is
en nou eers brand
littekensmompelstories
van reise wat nie gemeet kan word nie
na verdwyning wat nie geweet kan
    word nie

Seepunt, 7 Oktober 2015

HASSAN GHEDI SANTUR

Tell Me a Story

I T ALL STARTED with a simple request. "Tell me a story," she said.

It happened a few weeks ago. Khadija and Bashir had dinner at the long, mahogany table that was far too big for their small apartment and that looked even smaller thanks to their oversized sofas which had a tendency to swallow those unfortunate enough to sit on them.

"Tell me a story," Khadija said with a sigh that betrayed a quiet desperation.

She's already bored with me, Bashir thought to himself. But he obliged her anyway. Ever since she had told him she was pregnant, Bashir had become doting. Obsequious even. So he told her a story about how at age ten he went missing for two days. Walking home from school one day, he saw a lorry parked on the quiet dirt road that led to his home. He had always wanted to ride one, so he tightened his backpack around his shoulders and struggled to climb up onto it. As soon as he got into the back of the lorry, full of sacks of flour, the engine came to life. Elated by his first experience on a lorry as tall as a house,

HASSAN GHEDI SANTUR was born in Somalia and spent his formative years in Mogadishu. At age 14, he left Somalia with his family for what they thought would be a temporary trip. Not long after, the violent revolution that started in northern Somalia reached the capital and a 20-year civil war began. He settled in Toronto, Canada with his family. To learn English, he started reading voraciously and listening to public radio. He eventually earned a BA in English literature and an MFA in screenwriting at York University, embarking on a career in journalism as a freelancer, mostly for CBC Radio – to which incidentally he used to listen to in order to improve his English. In 2010, he published his debut novel *Something Remains* which was longlisted for the The ReLit Awards. After a year working in and traveling around East Africa, he relocated to New York City to pursue a Master's degree in Politics & Global Affairs at Columbia University Graduate School of Journalism. He recently completed his second novel *The Youth of God* and is currently working on a long-form reportage about the refugee crisis unfolding in Italy and France.

little Bashir lay down on one of the sacks of flour, facing up at the blue sky above, and watched the tree branches whizz by.

Bashir fell asleep. When he woke up, it was dark and the lorry was locked in a large garage among dozens of other lorries. At sunset the following day, exhausted, covered in flour, Bashir was brought home by the two drivers of the lorry. He ran into his mother's arms. She held him sobbing for what seemed like hours. At last, she let go, held his face in her hands and slapped him hard, then kissed him repeatedly on the forehead.

When Bashir finished telling his wife the story, he asked her to tell him a story about her childhood. And so she did. Sharing anecdotes and snapshots from their past became a nightly ritual. She told him about the day her best friend Fatima dared her to steal a bag of candy from a neighborhood store. Khadija got caught by the storeowner and taken to the police station.

Night after night, these storytelling sessions took place after dinner as they sipped tea or shared a bowl of vanilla ice cream like a new couple on a date.

Bashir poured some sesame oil into his palms, rubbed them together and began to massage his wife's feet. Khadija's feet had developed a tendency to swell as her pregnancy progressed. She lay on the couch, her back propped up with two pillows, and her feet in Bashir's lap. The television was on and Al-Jazeera English was showing a report about the worsening humanitarian situation in Syria.

"Ruffa?" Khadija said, unable to wrap her tongue around the name.

"No," Bashir said laughing. "Rufus." Lately he has gotten into the habit of suggesting strange names whenever she brought up the subject of what they would name the baby. Yesterday he told her that if the baby was a girl he wanted to name her Chaka, after his favorite soul singer Chaka Khan. She laughed hysterically and said over her dead body. Tonight he told her that if the baby was a boy, they should name him Rufus.

"Ruf-fus!" Khadija attempted to repeat. "People give their children such names?"

"Yes!" Bashir said emphatically. "There is a famous Canadian singer named Rufus."

"No. Really. No." Khadija said shaking her head. "It sounds like a dog's name."

Bashir laughed and nodded. They turned to the television in unison when they heard the newscaster suddenly mention Somalia.

Khadija reached for the remote and turned up the volume. She listened intently though she could not understand everything the newscaster was saying. Her eyes widened when she heard the name Kismaayo and she turned to Bashir with a worried look. It was his cue to start translating.

"Twenty-one people were killed yesterday, many of them civilians," Bashir said, translating simultaneously as he listened to the report. "The African Union troops supported by the Somali National Army have entered the coastal city that has been controlled by the Al-Qaeda-linked terrorist group Al-Shabaab. Thousands of civilians have fled to neighboring towns." Bashir continued his slow, methodical translation. He turned away from the TV to find his wife holding her hand to her mouth. "Do we have a calling card," she said. "We must call my father."

"It's three in the morning there, sweetie," Bashir said, reaching out to hold her hand. "We'll call them first thing in the morning."

Khadija didn't protest but she also didn't agree. She just sat there, her gaze fixed on the television screen even though the news had moved on to the war in Libya.

It had taken Khadija, her father and her sisters weeks to figure out the time difference between Toronto and Kismaayo. She used to call them at all hours of the day, sometimes waking her father at two in the morning and they too called her at all hours of the day, often rousing Bashir from the depths of sleep at four in the morning. And although Khadija's homesickness had abated somewhat, she still called her family almost every day. Bashir often pictured his wife's telephone conversation as a long, transatlantic umbilical cord that nourished her and any attempt on his part to sever it as likely to result in his wife's unraveling. So he learned to accept the late night calls as the price of admission into his wife's heart.

For many months after their wedding and after he had relocated Khadija to Toronto, Bashir felt shut out of his wife's interior world. It was as though she was punishing him for taking her so far away from the only place and people she had ever known and loved. His uncle Ahmed had told him some basic facts about her family. Simple background information like the fact that in 1993 when Khadija was only nine years old, a year-long drought had completely destroyed her family's banana farm, a misfortune from which her family never recovered and after which the country fell into the most severe famine in its recent history.

Bashir's uncle had also told him that Khadija had planned to marry Nuruddin, one of the boys in her neighborhood. He was a tall, broad-shouldered boy her own age whose dark, wavy hair and talent on the town's soccer field had all the girls swooning. But it was ultimately Khadija who captured the young man's heart. Bashir never found out the details of what happened to the life that Khadija had planned with Nuruddin except for a few cryptic sentences he had been able to coax out of her during his many attempts to get to know her better. He had almost given up all hope until very recently when Khadija had finally allowed her husband the access he had sought for the better part of their thirteen-month marriage.

A week ago, after making love, Bashir lay next to her with his arm around her neck, his hand resting on her warm, bare shoulder. "Can I ask you something?" he said with his eyes focused on the ceiling. Khadija's head lay on his chest, her fingers gently scratching the patch of hair on his chest. "Sure," she said, trying to suppress a yawn.

"Tell me about Nuruddin," Bashir heard himself say. He felt her body tense. From the periphery of his vision, he saw her lift her head a little and stare at him. He turned to her and saw in her eyes a look he had never seen before. A look that was at once wounded, confused, and offended but also intrigued. It was as though there was a small part of her that admired him for acknowledging that she had a life before him, a life that didn't include marrying him or migrating to Canada. Somewhere in her eyes, Bashir had also registered gratitude for understanding that she had made sacrifices to be with him.

Khadija reached for the lamp on the nightstand and turned off the light. In the dark, obscured from her husband, she told him the story of her love affair with Nuruddin. Freed by Bashir's audacious question, Khadija told him how she and Nuruddin met one day as she was carrying a large container full of water that she had walked thirty minutes to collect from a local pump that sold water whenever the tap water stopped. She told her husband of Nuruddin's cheeky humor and the slow evolution of their mutual love that was conducted in a secret rendezvous in the one cinema house in town that played Bollywood movies, where they sat next to each another, holding hands under her cotton *garbosaar*. And in a tone of a woman who had made peace with her fate, she told him of the day it all came to an end two years after the death of her mother Nadifa and the collapse of her father's latest foolhardy business venture. As the eldest of three siblings and with a father who couldn't take care of them, Khadija left school a year shy of her high school graduation. She took a job with a distant cousin who owned a store that made women's clothing. She didn't earn much but it was enough to help feed her younger sisters and send them to school.

Khadija showed no emotion when she told him about the night her father asked her to sit down next to him on the *sali* on which he prayed and asked her if she knew where Canada was. Her world geography wasn't great but she knew enough to understand that Canada was far away and cold. Her father told her that a man from Canada had asked to marry her. Khadija told her father she would rather marry Nuruddin. Her father said that wasn't an option and that marrying him would just be yet another mouth to feed. Her father, not a man to make demands or raise his voice, told her to think about the marriage proposal and what it would mean to her family and give him her final answer in three days.

Khadija stopped telling the story and cupped her husband's cheek in her palm. The meaning of this gesture confounded Bashir. Was it a gesture of sympathy for the husband to whom she was confiding her great love or was it intended to remind him of the sacrifices she had made to marry him? Bashir couldn't tell. "Then what happened?" he said. "Tell me the whole story."

"I knew what my answer would be even before my father finished his request. But I took the three days he gave me. On the third night when he came home, I brought him his dinner and sat on the edge of his *sali* and told him that I had my decision. I asked him if he would respect what I decide? He said yes without hesitation. I told him that I accept the proposal. He nodded, smiled and ate his dinner.

"Why did you say yes?"

Khadija was silent for a moment. Perhaps she was searching for the right words, the proper way to answer her husband without hurting his feelings.

"For my sisters," she said at last. "I did it for my sisters…I knew that what little money my father made wouldn't be enough to send my three sisters to school."

Bashir put his arm around his wife's shoulder as if to thank her for the decision she made. And a part of him was happy that she had said yes to his proposal not only because she was there with him, in bed, in the dark, her pregnant belly pressed against him. But also because he knew that at the end of every month when they got into their car and drove to Dahabshiil, the remittance bank on Weston Road, to send her father four hundred dollars, three young girls in Kismaayo would be going to school thanks to his wife's decision to marry him. And as he lay next to his wife, Bashir pictured her sisters sitting in three different classes in Horseed Private School. It was a small school for girls run by Halima Roble, a Somali woman with a Master's degree in education from the University of Reading in the U.K. who had moved back to her hometown to open a school for girls.

Khadija finished her story and rested her head on Bashir's chest. She remained quiet for a while until she cleared her throat and said, "now you."

"Now me what?"

Khadija pinched her husband's nipple. "Ouch!" he yelled and they both laughed.

"I told you mine. Now you tell me your story," she said.

In the darkness of their bedroom, Bashir felt his wife smile at him. He grinned incredulously as he considered her request. He debated just how much of his past it was wise to share with her. A part of him wanted to tell her everything, to come clean about the long parade of women, both Somalis and non-Somalis he had dated and slept with until his heart and his body had tired of the chase. But it wasn't until he felt the loss of that singular thrill of pulling down a new girl's panties, a thrill that had once motivated his every action, that he had decided to call his uncle Ahmed in Nairobi and accept his oft-repeated offer of facilitating a marriage to a "good Somali girl," as he put it. Perhaps it was the deep loneliness that had wrapped itself around him like a shawl or the fact that he was turning forty in a few months. Whatever the reason, Bashir picked up the phone one night and said the words his uncle had been waiting for. He still remembered the shock he felt as he hung up the phone, and the regret and confusion that had surged through him. He was stunned that he could cast away his many deeply held beliefs about romance, courtship, and the progress of love. He found it at once thrilling and unsettling that three months shy of forty, he still possessed the capacity to be shocked by his choices.

Bashir ignored his desire to confess everything and told his wife of the only one that really mattered. In details equaling hers, Bashir told his wife about Mikeila and about their deep and tumultuous three-year love affair that ended because of his inability or unwillingness to make himself vulnerable and take the risk of telling Mikeila how much he loved her. When Bashir finished telling his wife about Mikeila, Khadija didn't say anything. Bashir's heart began to beat fast and he instantly regretted his frankness. He berated himself for going along with his wife's nightly storytelling game. He had always suspected total honesty was never a good idea in a marriage and that night as he lay next to his wife who had suddenly gone mute on him, his suspicion was confirmed.

"You should've told her," Khadija said at last.

Bashir tilted his head a little to see her but it was too dark to see the expression on her face. "Told her what?"

"How much you loved her."

Now it was Bashir's turn to be mute. He didn't know what to say. So he remained silent and pulled her closer to him.

That night, as they lay in bed in the dark, unable to inspect each other's eyes, Khadija had, at last, allowed him in and given him the access into the interior recesses of her consciousness that he had yearned for. And in return, he had laid bare his regrets and the risks he never took for the woman he loved. And she had consoled him with a long, wet kiss on the mouth. As their evening storytelling ritual progressed, it became the part of Bashir's day that he looked forward to the most. It was also in another one of these nightly story-sharing sessions that his wife had told him the truth about the day her mother Nadifa walked into the Indian Ocean.

They had just finished watching another Bollywood film, a tragic story that ended with a young bride who kills herself with rat poison after her beloved is murdered by a ruthless gang leader in the slums of Mumbai. They lay on the couch, their limbs entangled. Khadija had the look of someone kicked in the gut. She had never told anyone the story of her mother's death. It was a secret her family had kept from their neighbors and even their closest relatives. In her world, suicide was a sin for which the survivors of the deceased were shunned as if the act of self-killing ran in the family like a curse. That night, Khadija finally shared with her husband the secret she carried with her from Kismaayo to Canada.

Khadija's mother Nadifa never recovered from the death of her twin boys Zakhariye and Ismail. When the great drought of 1993 hit, it destroyed the family's banana farm. Penniless and hungry, Nadifa knew their only chance of survival was to join the caravan of neighbors headed for a place called Dadaab somewhere in the northwest of Kenya. Khadija's father tried to dissuade his wife from the treacherous journey but Nadifa threatened she would take the kids and walk by herself. Her father relented and the entire family—Khadija, who was nine at the time, her younger sisters Filsan, Sameera, and Nuurto, as well as the twin boys—all set out on foot to take an uncertain chance at survival. The twin boys who were only ten months old were ill-prepared for the two-week foot journey through the parched lands of southern Somalia. A week into the trip, their soft bodies gave up. Their dehydrated corpses were buried at the foot of a leafless acacia tree, their graves unmarked.

Blaming herself for the loss of her only boys, the boys that would carry the family name, Nadifa fell into a deep and unrelenting depression. Even a year later when the family returned to their farm house in Kismaayo, Nadifa barely spoke or ate, her talent for reciting the melodic *Buraanbur* she was famous for, snuffed out by the weight of the guilt she carried like a thing around her neck. At the crack of dawn, on a beautiful sunny morning, three months after their return to Kismaayo, Nadifa put on her favorite white *guntiino* and told Khadija, who was sitting in the outdoor kitchen making breakfast, that she was going for a walk. She never returned. Three days later, the Indian Ocean spat Nadifa's bloated body onto the beach of a nearby village. She was still tangled in her white *guntiino* and long strands of seaweed.

Khadija cried as she finished telling her husband the story of her mother's death. Bashir put his arm around his wife and held her convulsing body as she sobbed. He held her until she stopped crying. As Bashir hugged her tight, he felt it at last. A year into their marriage, he had, at last, fallen in love with his wife.

"You know what hurts the most," Khadija said. Bashir shook his head.

"When I think of my mom now, I don't think of her sardonic sense of humor or her great intellect. I don't hear her melodic voice that made her *baraanbur* so beautiful to listen to. I don't see the high cheekbones I used to covet so much. The only thing that comes to my mind when I think of her now is this image and I don't even know where it comes from. It's not like I was there to witness it." Khadija was quiet for a moment as if to conjure up an image long repressed. "I see her walking toward the water's edge, her back turned to me. Her white *guntiino* is blowing in the wind as she walks into the dark blue water. I call out to her but she doesn't turn back. She just walks further and further into the ocean until she is submerged." Khadija paused for a moment. "That's the only thing that comes to my mind when I think of my mother . . . Isn't that terrible?"

"There was more to her life than the way it ended," Bashir said as he took his wife's hand and held it to his lips.

"I have this fantasy sometimes. I think about my whole family in heaven. My dad, my sisters, and the twins, still babies. We're all chatting and laughing together in paradise remembering funny things that happened in Kismaayo. Except for my mom. She is not with us. She's not with us because people who kill themselves don't go to heaven. They go to hell."

"We don't know that."

"That's what the Qur'an says. Allah punishes them with eternity in hell."

"Allah also forgives. He's the most merciful. Most forgiving. The Qur'an tells us that repeatedly."

Khadija remained quiet for a long time as if counting the number of times the Qur'an calls Allah the most merciful. Most compassionate. Most forgiving.

Hassan Hajjaj,
Kesh Angels, 2010

ALFRED SCHAFFER

Translated from the Dutch by MICHELLE HUTCHINSON

Man Animal Thing

ALFRED SCHAFFER (1973) is a poet and translator. He works as a lecturer in the department of Afrikaans and Netherlands at the University of Stellenbosch. He made his poetry debut in 2000 in the Netherlands. His latest volume is titled *Mens Dier Ding* (*Man Animal Thing*, 2014). He has translated the poetry of South African poets Ronelda S. Kamfer, Antjie Krog and Charl-Pierre Naudé. He lives in Cape Town.

MICHELLE HUTCHISON is a translator and editor living in Amsterdam. She mainly translates from Dutch and covers several genres from poetry to graphic novels to fiction and non-fiction. Her translation of Esther Gerritsen's *Craving* was shortlisted for the 2015 Vondel Prize. Recent publications include *La Superba* by Ilja Leonard Pfeijffer, *Fortunate Slaves* by Tom Lanoye and *How To Talk About Places You've Never Been* by Pierre Bayard.

dag(droom) # 5.106

De klassieke shoot-out.
En dat met zoveel concurrentie
niet normaal, mijn ballen tintelen
    ervan.
Aan de ene kant sta ik en aan de
    andere kant
daar sta ik ook, maar dan de uitgele-
    kte en verkouden versie.
De albinosmurf die uit De Smurfen
    werd geknipt
en uit ik weet niet wat.
De spanning knettert als de brand in

Day(Dream) # 5,106

The classic shoot-out.
And with so much competition too
it's bizarre, it makes my balls tingle.
I stand on one side and on the other
    side
there's me too, only the leaked
    version with a cold.
The albino smurf cut out of The
    Smurfs
and somewhere else I forgot.
Tension crackles like a fire in a paper
    factory.

een papierfabriek.
Ik kijk nog een keer heel precies –
wat ben ik dik geworden,
        allemachtig, stevig sta ik niet.
Als een dictator op sterk water.
Tussen ons een mateloze vlakte, een
        betonnen poolgebied.
Eigenlijk gewoon een mix van zand
        en gras
niet groter dan de achtertuin waarin
        ik vroeger lag.
Ik zie me denken Maar dat ís mijn
        lichaam niet
dat bén ik niet, nooit zou ik naar
        mijn vestzak tasten
om mijn mondharmonica te pakken
en een onverstandig deuntje te gaan
        fluiten.

I take another really good look –
how fat I've become, god almighty,
        I'm not solid.
Like a dictator in formaldehyde.
Between us a boundless expanse, a
        concrete polar region.
Actually just a mixture of sand and
        grass
no larger than the back garden I used
        to lie in.
I see myself thinking but that's not
        my body
that's not me, I would never grope
        around my jacket pocket
for a mouth organ
to play a foolish little tune on.

Sjaka's korte flirt met romantiek

Op een dag verscheen hij als verschi-
    jning aan haar deur.
Het moet zijn eerste en zijn laatste
    poging zijn geweest.
Bosje bloemen in de hand, wat rozen
    en chrysanten
schone rook blies uit de rookmachine
    achter hem
en bungelend aan touwen het heelal
bewust apolitiek en stralend.
Het had een cent gekost en flink wat
    logistiek
en bloedvergieten, maar zijn
    voorpret
richtte het vizier op het spektakel in
    haar bed.
Had men hem wat dan ook geflikt
op dat moment, standvastig was hij
    blijven staan.
Klopte aan en nog een keer en nog
    maar eens.

Shaka's Brief Flirtation with Romance

One day he appeared at her door like
    an apparition.
It must have been his first and last
    attempt.
Bunch of flowers in his hand, some
    roses and chrysanthemums
clean smoke blowing out of the
    smoke machine behind him
and the universe dangling on ropes
consciously apolitical and shining.
It had cost a pretty penny, some
    serious logistics
and bloodshed, but his anticipatory
    pleasure
set its sights on the spectacle in her
    bed.
If anyone had tried to pull one over
    on him
at that moment, he would have
    stood his ground.

Wat bleek na enig overleg
hij stond voor het verkeerde huis!
Onderdanen gleden lacherig en
    ongelovig
uit de bomen, ramen werden weer
    gesloten
ook de dames van de drumband
    maakten rechtsomkeert.
Geruisloos werd hij weggeleid
een afgeleefde aak in een immens
    kanaal
en men vergat die hele zaak opdat
    dit nooit
en nooit weer zou gebeuren.

Knocked and then again and then
    again.
After some discussion it turned out
he was at the wrong house!
Laughing in disbelief, locals slid
down from the trees, windows were
    closed again
even the ladies from the drum band
    made an about turn.
He was led off silently
a decrepit barge in an immense canal
and people forgot about the whole
    business so that it
would never happen again.

'zelfportret als 007' – dag(droom) # 1.516

Er is iets fout gegaan.
Ik hang als aangeschoten wild veel
    wind te vangen
hoog boven een stad.
Kantoorglas overal, het bloed trekt
    langzaam uit mijn armen.
In de verte fikt wat na, een groepje
    honden
staat beneden op het asfalt woest te
    blaffen
helikopters hangen ratelend als sla-
    groomkloppers buiten beeld.
Tot nu toe deed ik al mijn eigen
    stunts.
Ik slaak wat kreten die niet in het
    draaiboek staan
dat ik het kwaad met kwaad bestreed
het kwaad was als een kakkerlak.
Ik kwam geroepen als altijd
om in de slotminuten triomfantelijk
    de toekomst in te wandelen
mijn daden en mijn misdaden ver-
    geven en vergeten –
nooit sprak ik mijn mond voorbij
ik liet nog liever los.

'Self-portrait as 007' – Day(Dream) # 1,516

Something has gone wrong.
I hang like shot game catching copious
    amounts of wind
high above a city.
Office glass everywhere, the blood
    slowly leaves my arms.
Something burning in the distance, a
    pack of dogs
bark angrily on the asphalt down below
helicopters hover out of sight rattling
    like egg whips.
Up to now, I'd always done my own
    stunts.
I utter a few screams that aren't in the
    script
that I fought evil with evil
evil was like a cockroach.
I always turned up when needed
before wandering off triumphantly into
    the future during the
closing scenes
my deeds and misdeeds forgiven and
    forgotten –
I never shot my mouth off
I'd rather let go.

Sjaka Vindt Uiteindelijk De Liefde Van Zijn Leven

in een modetijdschrift van zijn moeder.
Die ogen en die kleine kin, die juk-
    beenderen!
Noemt haar N, hoe moet hij haar
    omschrijven.
Als een wandeling bij avond na een
    feeërieke film.
Als een rit in zijn aftandse kever
tussen rotsachtig gebergte, hij sling-
    ert langs een rimpelloze beek
en plotseling breekt de zon door
breekt het zonlicht door de ruimte,
    diep beneden
ligt het dal waar hij zal blijven slapen.
N! Als een abrupte smaak die losbarst
    in je mond
een stortbui in het hartje van de zomer.
Verslavend als een voetbalspelletje.
Sleetse beeldspraak klaagt zijn
    biograaf maar Ach
zolang het werkt, denkt Sjaka.

Shaka Finally Finds The Love Of His Life

in one of his mother's fashion
    magazines.
Those eyes and that small chin, those
    cheekbones!
Calls her N, how should he describe
    her?
Like an evening stroll after a magical
    film
Like a drive in a dilapidated Beetle
between rocky mountains, he meanders
    along a glassy stream
and suddenly the sun breaks through
the sunlight breaks through the air,
    far below
is the valley where he will spend the
    night.
N! Like an abrupt taste that explodes
    in your mouth
heavy rain at the height of summer.
As addictive as a football game.
His biographer complains of

Die zo argeloos vermorzelt maar niet
  dansen kan.
Die steeds weer op de tenen van zijn
  partner trapt.
Heeft geen idee hoe hij een drankje
  aan moet bieden
hoe je met je hele mond moet zoenen.
Als kleine jongen werd hij met de
  liefde vaak gepest.
'Dikke Babette gaat met Sjaka naar bed'
en 'Sjaka = Nerd' stond met koeien-
  letters
op de zijmuur van de buurtwinkel
  geschreven.
Giftig rende hij naar huis, verborg zich
op zijn kamertje en kwam er dagen-
  lang niet uit.

Geconcentreerd slijpt hij de punt bij
  van zijn speer
en vraagt zich af of N van zijn
  bestaan afweet.
Of hij haar in haar dromen uit de
  vlammen redt
en of zij starend naar zijn foto wat
  parfum

hackneyed imagery, never mind
as long as it works, Shaka thinks.
Who crushes so guilelessly but
  cannot dance.
Who keeps treading on his partner's
  toes.
Has no idea how to offer a drink
how to kiss with your whole mouth.
As a young boy he was often teased
  about love.
'Fat Babette is shagging Shaka'
and 'Shaka = Nerd' in giant letters
on the side wall of the corner shop.
Bitter, he ran home, hid
  himself away
in his bedroom and didn't come out
  for days.

He concentrates on sharpening the
  point of his spear
and wonders whether N knows that
  he exists.
Whether in her dreams he rescues
  her from the flames
and whether she sprays a little
  perfume between her breasts

tussen haar borsten spuit, het eten
    aan laat branden
met make-up haar oneffenheden
    wegpoetst
terwijl ze "They can't take that away
    from me" neuriet.

Radeloos van ongeleid verlangen
begeeft hij zich zo'n vier keer in de
    week
richting de roodverlichte achter-
    straten van het dorp.
Dan blijft hij weg tot hij geen cent
    meer heeft.
Ver na middernacht zwalkt hij nog
    over straat.
In een leven van minuut tot minuut
op weg naar meer en steeds meer leven.

---

while looking at his photo, leaves the
    dinner to burn
disguises her imperfections with
    make-up
while humming "They can't take that
    away from me."

About four times a week and
crazy with longing
    he heads towards
the red-lit backstreets of the village.
He stays there until he hasn't a
    cent left.
Long after midnight he's still
    roaming the streets.
Living from minute to minute
on his way to more and still
    more life.

SANMAO

Translated from the Chinese by MIKE FU

Desert Dining

SANMAO (1943–1991) was a novelist, travel writer, translator, and screenwriter. Her pseudonym was adopted from a character from acclaimed caricaturist Zhang Leping's most famous work, entitled *Sanmao*. She studied philosophy at the Chinese Culture University in Taiwan, later moving to Germany and then back to Taiwan. In 1976 she published the autobiographical work *The Stories of the Sahara*, which was about her experiences living in then Spanish-controlled Western Sahara with her Spanish husband José. Part travelogue and part memoir, it is an account of life and love in the desert, and quickly established Sanmao as a writer with a unique voice and perspective. Following the book's immense success in Taiwan, Mainland China, as well as Hong Kong, her early writings were collected in a second book, published under the title *Gone with the Rainy Season*. In 1991, at the age of 47, Sanmao died in a hospital in Taipei, having hung herself with a pair of silk stockings.

I T'S TOO BAD my husband is a foreigner. Referring to my own husband as such undoubtedly seems a bit exclusive. But since every country has language and customs completely unlike the next, there are some areas in our conjugal life where it's impossible to see eye to eye. When I first agreed to marry José, I reminded him that we differed not only in nationality but in personality. Perhaps one day we might even argue to the point of physical confrontation. He replied, "I know you can be moody but you've got a good heart. Fight as we may, let's get married anyway." So we finally tied the knot seven years after we first met.

I wouldn't call myself a feminist, but I wasn't willing to toss aside the carefree spirit of my independence. I made extra clear that I would still do things my way after marriage. Otherwise we could scrap the whole idea. José told me, "All I want is for you to do things your way. If you lost your individuality and flair, I wouldn't see any point in marrying you!" Great to hear such things from the big guy himself. I was very pleased.

As the wife of José, I oblige him in terms of language. My poor foreigner, he still can't tell the difference between the Chinese characters for "person" and "enter" no matter how many times I teach him. I let him off easy and speak his language instead. (But once we have children, they'll learn Chinese if it kills them. He's all in favor of this idea too.)

Let's be real: the housewife's top priority is the kitchen. I've always loathed chores, but cooking is something I take great pleasure in. Give me some scallions and a few slices of meat and I can whip up a dish like that. I quite relish this form of artistry.

My mother in Taiwan was devastated when she found out that I was going to the barrens of Africa because of José's work. José is the breadwinner around here so I had to follow my meal ticket. No room for argument there. Our kitchen was dominated by Western food in those early days of marriage. But then assistance came to our household via airmail. I received vermicelli, seaweed, shiitake mushrooms, instant noodles, dried pork, and other valuable foodstuffs in bulk. I was so overjoyed I couldn't keep my hands off. Add to that list a jug of soy sauce sent by a girlfriend in Europe, and the Chinese restaurant in our household was just about ready for business. A pity there was only one nonpaying customer to be had. (Eventually we had friends lining up at the door to come eat!)

Actually, what my mother sent me really wasn't enough to run a Chinese restaurant, but luckily José had never been to Taiwan. He saw that I had the cockiness of a master chef and began to take confidence in me.

The first dish was chicken soup with vermicelli. Whenever he gets home from work, José always yells, "Hurry up with dinner, I'm starving!" All those years of being loved by him for naught. He clamors for food without even giving me a second glance. At least I won't have to worry about my looks going. Anyway, back to that chicken soup and vermicelli. He took a sip and asked, "Hey, what's this? Thin Chinese noodles?"

"Would your mother-in-law send thin noodles from such incredible distances? No way."

"Well, what is it, then? I want some more. It's delicious."

I picked up a noodle with my chopsticks. "This? It's called 'rain.'"

"Rain?" He was dumbfounded.

Like I said, I do as I please in marriage and say things impulsively for fun. "This is from the first rainfall of the spring. After the mountain rain freezes over, the natives tie it up and take it down to sell in bundles and buy rice wine. It's not easy to come by!"

José still had a blank expression on his face. He scrutinized me, then the "rain" in his bowl, and said, "You think I'm an idiot?"

I brushed his question aside. "You still want some more?"

"I still do, you goddamn liar," he answered. Afterward he would often eat this "spring rain" and to this day he still doesn't know what it's made from. Sometimes I feel sad that José can be so stupid.

The second time we had vermicelli with ground meat. I fried the noodles in a saucepan, then sprinkled shredded meat and juice on top. José is always hungry when he comes home from work. He chomped right into the noodles. "What's this? It looks like white yarn or plastic."

"It's neither," I replied. "It's nylon like the fishing line you use, made white and soft by Chinese labor."

He had another mouthful and gave me a small smile. Still chewing, he said, "So many weird things. If we really opened a restaurant, we'd have to sell this

MIKE FU is a Brooklyn-based writer and translator. He received his MA in East Asian Languages and Cultures from Columbia University and MFA in Creative Writing and Literary Translation from Queens College, City University of New York. He has translated screenplays, treatments, subtitles, and other material for contemporary Chinese filmmakers including Huang Weikai and Li Ning.

one at a good price, my little one." That day he ate his fill of upgraded nylon.

The third time we had vermicelli with spinach and meat, all minced very fine, inside a Northeastern-style bun. He said, "You put shark fin in this little bun, right? I heard this thing is pretty expensive. No wonder you only put in a little." I laughed myself to the floor. "Tell your mom not to buy any more of this expensive shark fin for us. I want to write her to say thanks."

I was deeply amused. "Go write her now, I'll translate! Ha!"

One day, around the time José got off work, I remembered that he hadn't seen the dried pork yet. I pulled it out of hiding and cut it into little squares with scissors. Then I put the pieces in a jar and bundled it in a blanket. It just so happened that he was a little congested that day and wanted to bring out an extra blanket for bed. I was sitting nearby reading Water Margin for the thousandth time, having forgotten about my treasure for the moment. He lay in bed with the jar in his hands, peering at it left and right.

When I looked up, my goodness! It was like when they discovered King Solomon's treasure. I snatched it from him and said, "This isn't for you to eat. It's medicine… Chinese medicine."

"My nose is all stuffed up, so this medicine will be perfect." He had already put a handful into his mouth. I was furious, but kept silent since I couldn't demand that he spit it out. "It's pretty sweet. What is it?"

"Lozenges," I snapped. "To soothe a cough."

"Lozenges made from meat? You think I'm an idiot?"

The next day, I discovered that he had taken more than half of the jar's contents to share with his co-workers. From that day onward, his co-workers would always pretend to cough when they saw me, hoping to extort some dried pork slices.

In any case, married life is all about eating. The rest of the time is spent making money in order to eat. There really isn't much more to it. One day I made rice balls, or sushi, you could say, with rice and dried shredded meat wrapped in seaweed. This time José refused to eat it.

"What? You're actually giving me carbon paper to eat?"

I asked him gently, "You really won't eat it?"

"No, no way."

Excellent. I was more than happy to eat a pile myself.

"Open your mouth and let me see!" he demanded.

"See, there's no color stain. I used the opposite side of the roll of carbon paper. It won't dye your mouth." I was used to bluffing every day, so I could easily come up with this kind of nonsense.

"You're a damn liar, that's what you are. I hate you. Tell me the truth, what is it?"

"You have no clue about China," I replied, eating another roll. "I'm so disappointed in my husband."

He got mad and snatched up a roll with his chopsticks. Adopting the expression of a tragic hero embarking upon a path of no return, he chewed and chewed and swallowed. "Yep, it's seaweed."

I jumped up and exclaimed, "Yes, you got it! You're so smart!" I was about to jump again when I received a hard flick on the head from him.

When we had eaten most of the Chinese things, I grew reluctant to serve from my Chinese restaurant. Western dishes came back to the table. José was really surprised but happy to see me making steak when he came home from work. "Make mine medium rare. And are you frying potatoes too?"

After we had steak three days in a row, he seemed to have lost his appetite.

He would stop eating after just one bite.

"Are you too tired from work? Do you want to sleep for a bit, then eat later?" Even this old lady can still play tender.

"I'm not sick. I just think we're not eating well."

Upon hearing this, I bounded up with a roar. "Not eating well? Not eating well? Do you know how much this steak costs per pound?"

"It's not that, my dear wife. I want to have some of that 'rain.' The food your mom sent us tastes better."

"Alright then, our Chinese restaurant will operate twice a week. How about it? How often do you want it to rain?"

One day, José came home and said to me, "The big boss called me in today."

"A pay raise?" My eyes lit up.

"No—"

"No?" I grabbed him, sinking my nails into his flesh. "Did you get fired? Oh, we're doomed! Oh my God, we—"

"Let go of me, you psycho. Let me finish. The big boss said that everyone at the company has been over to eat at our house except for him and his wife. He's waiting for you to invite him over for Chinese—"

"The big boss wants me to cook for him? I won't do it! Don't invite him. I'll happily do it for any of your colleagues, but it's unethical to invite your superior. I'm a person of integrity, you know, I—" I wanted to go on about the moral character of the Chinese people, but I couldn't explain it clearly. Then I saw the expression on José's face and realized I could only choke down my morality.

The next day, he asked me, "Hey, do we have any bamboo shoots?"

"Plenty of chopsticks in the house, all made out of bamboo."

He gave me a dirty look. "The big boss wants bamboo shoots with shiitake mushrooms."

Amazing. This boss has truly been all over the world. Can't underestimate these foreigners. "Alright, invite the two of them over for dinner tomorrow night. I'll come up with some bamboo shoots, no problem." José looked over at me with great affection. It was the first time he'd looked at me like this since we got married. What a rare favor bestowed upon me! Too bad my hair was a tangled mess and I looked like death that day.

The following night, I prepared three dishes ahead of time and kept them warmed at a simmer. I set up the dinner table with a red cloth diagonally over-laying a white cloth, and a candle holder on top. It was a lovely arrangement. Everyone enjoyed themselves thoroughly at the meal. Not only were the dishes perfect in presentation, aroma, and taste, I had also cleaned myself up nicely and went so far as to put on a long skirt.

When the boss and his wife were getting ready to leave, they told me, "If we ever have an opening in public relations, we hope you can fill in and be a part of the company." My eyes gleamed with joy. All this thanks to bamboo shoots with shiitake mushrooms.

It was already late after we sent them off. I immediately took off the long skirt in favor of a pair of ripped jeans. Tying my hair up with some bands, I began furiously washing bowls and plates. I felt so much more at ease, both physically and spiritually, back in my Cinderella getup.

José was quite satisfied. He asked from behind, "Hey, the bamboo shoots and mushrooms were really great. Where'd you get the bamboo?"

Continuing with the dishes, I asked, "What bamboo?"

"The bamboo shoots from tonight's dinner!"

I cracked up. "Oh, you mean the cucumber stirfried with mushroom?"

"What? You… You can fool me all you want, but you dare pull that on the boss–"

"I didn't fool him. It was the most delicious meal of bamboo shoots stirfried with shiitake mushrooms he's ever had. He said so himself."

José scooped me up in his arms, getting soapy water all over his head and beard. He said, "You're the greatest! The greatest! You're like that monkey, the one with seventy-two transformations. What was his name? What…?"

I patted his head. "The Great Sage, Equal of Heaven, Sun Wukong! Don't go forgetting his name this time."

TAREK ELTAYEB
Translated from the Arabic by KAREEM JAMES ABU-ZEID

هُدهُد

A Hoopoe

A garden sinks to sand
Surrenders to the locusts
So the hoopoe takes its leave

It flies south
Across tearing winds
In hopes of magic and feasting

It flies north
And they imprison it in a classroom
Where students draw its picture
Then they lure it to a museum
So it takes flight

It flies for days in darkness
Back to the garden
To its dunes and palms

وبستانٌ يَخِرُّ للرَّمّلِ

يستسلمُ للْجَرَادِ

فيستأذنُ الْهُدْهُدُ في الرَّحيل

يمرُقُ للجَنُوبِ

عَبْرَ رماحِ التَّمْزِيقِ

من أجْلِ سِحْرٍ ووليمةْ

يمرقُ للشَّمَالِ

فَيَحْبِسُونَهُ في قاعَةِ دَرسٍ

يرسُمُهُ فيها الطُّلَّابُ

ثم يُغْرُونَهُ بعملٍ في متحفْ

فيفرّ

يمرقُ طيَّارًا أيامًا

في ظلامٍ حتى الْبُستانِ

وأكوامِ الرَّمّلِ

TAREK ELTAYEB was
born to Sudanese parents in
Cairo in 1959. He has been
living in Vienna since 1984.
After studying at the Institute
for Economic Philosophy of
Vienna's University of Econom-
ics, he is currently teaching at
three universities in Austria.
He has been writing since
1985 and has published three
novels, two collections of
short stories, five collections
of poems, one play, one auto-
biographical book, and one
book of essays. His books have
been published in German,
English, Italian, French, Span-
ish, Macedonian, Romanian
and Serbian translations.
He is also a faculty member
of the International Writing
Program "Between the Lines"
at the University of Iowa.
His awards include the Elias
Cannetti Fellowship from the
City of Vienna (2005), and the
International Grand Prize for
Poetry from the 2007 Interna-
tional Festival Curtea de Argeş
in Romania.

It bemoans its lost wisdom
There's nothing left
Its heritage is lost
And one question follows the other

Will it pursue the sun?*

It is said that the sun set in the south
that day then rose in the north the
next, perplexing the creatures of the
world.

Will it rise with it at dawn?
In its grief and doubt
It sees a flock of birds on high
They cry out for it to rise
But its wings are weary:
It has nothing left
But the pretext
Of a farewell on two feet
And a steady plume

(Vienna, February 3, 2001)

والْخُوصِ الْمَدْفُون

يتحسَّرُ على زَمَانِ حِكْمَتِه

لا شَيْءَ في شَيْءٍ

ميراثُه ضائعٌ

أسئلةٌ تَنْسَخُ أسئلة

أيتبع شمسًا بعد رحيل*؟

أم يُشرق معَها في الفجر؟

في حَيْرَةِ حِسْبتِهِ وأسَاه

يمُرُّ عليه سِرْبُ طُيورٍ في العالي

تصيحُ إليهِ بأنْ يصعَدَ

لكنَّ جناحَيْهِ قد وَهَنا

ما عَادَ لهُ سِوَى

حجَّةِ وَدَاعٍ

على القدمَيْنِ

وريشةٍ صالحة

(فيينَا، 2001.2.3)

---

*It is said that the sun will set in the south that day then rise in the
north the next, perplexing the creatures of the world.

*يُقال إنّ الشمسَ في ذاك اليوم قد جنـبَت في الغروب، وفي اليوم التالي شمَّلت فاختار الخلق.

Stars

A calm child
Spoke softly
To the stars

He grew up

His voice grew coarse
The stars fell
Onto his shoulders
His feet grew heavy
As did his heart
As did his voice

(Vienna, December 5, 1995)

نجـومٌ

طفلاً وديعًا كان

يُنَاغِي النجومَ

بعذوبةٍ

طالَ

اخْشَنَ منهُ الصَّوْتُ

سقطَتْ نجومُه

على كتفيهِ

ثقُـلَتْ خُطاهُ

قلبَهُ

صوتَـهُ

(فِيِينـًا، 1995.12.5)

KAREEM JAMES ABU-ZEID has translated novels and books of poetry by Rabee Jaber, Najwan Darwish, Dunya Mikhail, and Tarek Eltayeb for NYRB Classics, New Directions, and AUC Press. His translations have won *Poetry Magazine*'s Translation Prize and a Northern California Book Award, have been longlisted for the National Translation Award and the Best Translated Book Award, and been Runner-up for the Banipal Translation Prize. He has been awarded residencies from the Lannan Foundation and the Banff Centre for the Arts, and has received a Fulbright Fellowship (Germany) and a CASA Fellowship (Egypt). He will be completing his PhD in Comparative Literature from UC Berkeley in summer 2016. He also translates from French and German.

Birth

She is
On the verge of death

He is
On the verge of life

Through their cries
In the cramped room
They share life
And shake off death

(*Vienna, May 7, 2001*)

ولادة

على حَافَّةِ الموتِ

هي

هو

على حَافَّةِ الحياةِ

بِصَرَخَاتِهِمَا

داخلَ الْغُرْفَةِ الضيقة

يتقاسمان الحياةَ

من الموتِ

(فيينــَا، 2001.5.7)

DIEKOYE OYEYINKA

Stillborn
(an excerpt)

Zombie
(Southern Nigeria, 2003)

DIEKOYE OYEYINKA spent his first fifteen years in Nigeria, and the next ten years between Europe and the USA. He has a B.A. in Economics from Georgetown University and a Master's degree in Urbanization and Development from the London School of Economics. His first novel, *Stillborn*, was published in Kenya in 2014 by East African Educational Publishers Ltd. Narrated from the point of view of Seun, an orphan from the Niger Delta who has been educated in the United States and is deciding whether or not he wants permanently to return to Lagos, *Stillborn* follows five characters whose lives intersect, taking the reader on a panoramic yet intimate journey through more than fifty years of Nigeria's turbulent history from independence in 1960 until the present. Oyeyinka says, "The specific inspiration for this book came from a deep-seated frustration with a broken system that was making false promises. I document the mistakes of the past so we do not blindly repeat them. The book is a memo to our leaders that we remember even after the headlines have faded." He lives in Lagos.

T HIS IS THE eternally enshrined image I have of my mother, Mrs. Ranti Ehurere. She wears her favorite bubu, its yellow and black streaks sit elegantly on her slender shoulders. She wears no jewelry on her neck—it is a work of art in itself. Her proud chin quivers as she talks incessantly. Her svelte fingers grip mine tightly, but I look away, embarrassed by her penetrating charcoal stare, her prescient tears streaming from ignorant eyes.

I had already been in Lagos for over five years, and each time I returned, Mother cried like it was the first time. Her unrestrained wails were the despondent soundtrack to Sagamu's rapidly fading lush scenery. But this time was different, I had come home for the long holiday before the final senior secondary school examinations, and mother had gotten used to my presence. She realized my childhood was ending, and she had missed a significant part of it. Once more, she was returning with me, and this time she did not attempt to camouflage her sorrow. Our arrival was like a déjà vu of the first, except I now walked with the assured steps of someone who had arrived home. Mother noticed this and it saddened her because each time I came to visit in the Niger Delta, I moved with the cautious gait of an intruder and opened drawers with the timidity of a guest. I promptly went upstairs to take a shower, and although I had bathed with a bucket and bowl until five years earlier, I felt I needed the stinging sprays on my body to wash away the products of three months of improper hygiene.

Mother and Uncle barely exchanged pleasantries before politics hijacked their discussions. It consumed every home in Nigeria and was present at every meal. Uncle had spent a lifetime crusading against the tyranny of military governance, and now the last and worst of the official dictators had died unexpectedly. The corpse was long buried, but juicy details still emerged casting a surreal light on the death and prompting renewed rounds of dinner table discussions.

"I hear he was killed by prostitutes," Mother said in disbelief.

"I am sure the CIA was involved," Uncle returned in a quiet voice, as though someone was listening. "I mean how could both Abacha and Abiola, the dictator and the president elect, both die mysteriously within the same month?"

"Let's just hope this Obasanjo knows what he is doing," mother replied. "He was once a military man."

"He still is one!" Uncle retorted. "The other day he told a senator to shut up. In my opinion we are still under military governance, especially if this party stays in power."

"Only God will help us," mother said tiredly.

Uncle smiled at this. He was tired of people sitting back with arms folded as the country fell apart, waiting on divine intervention. But he knew mother and father did what they could so he let the statement pass.

"But how is your side?" Uncle asked suddenly with obvious concern. "The place must be in shambles again. I thought you were approaching some calm finally after the Saro-Wiwa disaster, but these militants have turned the place upside down once more."

"I know you people fought Abacha from here, but you should have seen the area after they hung Ken and the other Ogoni leaders. I could only thank God that at least Seun was in school here."

"My dear, I know," Uncle said, "remember I visited. So, what is happening now with these militants? I am unsure if they are fighting against the state as the government claims or for the people as they say. I never trust armed uprisings."

"And it is the government you trust?" Mother retorted.

"Well, I also do not trust military rulers that return as civilians. So which is the frying pan and which is the fire?" Uncle asked.

"We will wait and see *o jare*. I am tired of these people and their *wahala*, all of them," she said, throwing her hand up in exasperation.

"So the militants are causing more trouble?" Uncle asked as though he already knew the answer.

"Some of them started nobly, but as usual the politicians have gotten their fingers into the water and muddied it."

"You mean the politicians are involved?" Uncle asked with disbelief.

"Of course nothing can be proven, but suddenly these militants went from disgruntled men protesting oil spills to young boys carrying machine guns siphoning oil and kidnapping as they wish. I'm sure you heard of the twelve murdered policemen."

"So who is involved?"

"That is what we don't know. But I am worried, because even if the federal government is profiting, they will not turn a blind eye and there will be retaliation soon. Obasanjo has been rather truculent about his plans to handle the issue. He has given the community leaders only a few days to produce the culprits"

"You see Seun is having a good time here. In fact tell your stubborn husband that he should take a break, and you should all come up here for a while," Uncle said, trying to change the mood.

Mother chuckled, "see you, you want us to completely take over your house, you have already been very gracious with Seun. He seems to be enjoying himself. And who is this Aisha girl he keeps talking about?"

"I think your boy has a crush. She is this Hausa girl next door. If you stayed longer, you would have met her," Uncle ventured in a last bid to extend her stay.

"You know your friend. That last time I was here and he did not see his wife for one week, you'd have thought the world was about to end." She said it with the happy sigh of a woman who believed a wife's place was by her husband's side. "Seun better not fall in love with a Hausa girl oh," mother was saying when Uncle's laugh cut her short.

"And look who is talking. Where is your husband from? The man does not even understand *ekaro*?" And they both laughed.

The purity of the untainted blue sky made my mother happy. Everything else was polluted—the water, the trees, the pleasures. The roads were mud, the houses were bare cement, and people cooked with crude firewood contraptions. She kept her eyes to the sky, trying to forget that just one week earlier she had left me behind in Lagos under a sky that leaked continuously like her eyes. The riots were unrelenting, and my father was convinced the government and multinationals would be forced to acquiesce to their demands. He refused to listen when he was told to stay home during the melees and mother was worried.

When they reasoned with him that as one of the organizers he should stay safe, he simply laughed and carried on in his quiet stubbornness. "The government will come to negotiate soon," he would say. "I must be there to welcome them."

A few kilometers away, a silver frog was serenading in burps from a black lake. Another drowned in a tar pond attended by large dragonflies with too many wings. Mother decided to do the laundry to distract her mind and carried a pale green bucket outside. She called repeatedly for my sister to bring some detergent and realized her voice was too loud. She stopped yelling and listened, it was much too quiet, and she looked around slightly disoriented.

Suddenly a loud boom was heard and the air exploded in a thousand lights, arousing the few animals left in the dying forests into coordinated cacophony. The bucket dropped from her hand and she ran towards the main road, unthinking, heading towards the sound. She had a feeling her daughter was there, she knew her husband was. She burst onto the road and was overwhelmed by the chaos: stones and bottles were being hurled at soldiers, and in return, they sent bullets and bombs. My mother, Mrs. Ranti Ehurere, died quickly and painlessly five minutes after she heard the first blast, and it was best.

It was best because she did not see her eight-year-old daughter pinned down by a sneering soldier as he slapped her roughly and raped her maliciously. She did not see the second soldier do the same and then shatter her skull with the butt of his gun. She did not see her husband's giant frame expire slowly as the hasty bullets of an automatic gutted his stomach, leaking acid on his large fingers as they tried to save his slowly expiring soul.

She did not see the crying old women as they rolled around on the floor repeatedly hitting their heads against the bloody mud. She did not see her neighbor curled in the fetal position in the pool of blood of her dead baby that she still clutched to her breast. The indiscriminate boots that trampled down doors and the impartial bullets that met whatever was behind them. She did not see her house in flames or the blackened remnants when the merciful acid rains finally came. She was not there when I heard the news, and she did not sit by my bed for six months. She did not see the sad makeshift tents of nylon and old sack that housed the survivors. She did not see our entire town burned to the ground. It was best that she did not hear the sad excuses the government gave for the massacre at Odi in Bayelsa state. The verdict of the military tribunals was always the same; the mayhem was committed by "unknown soldiers."

In the background, the streams of oil continued spurting out the black gold, but the dollars flowed not into the Central Bank but into the politicians' pockets, as the gas flares blazed at the top of long poles waving like the flags of the oil multinationals. The militant camps flooded with disenchanted youth anxious for the drugs that made them numb and the guns that gave false strength. In the capital, Governor O.C. Abari congratulated himself for getting his first hole-in-one on his personal golf course.

I was playing ludo with Aisha when Mrs. Folayo walked in. I had just rolled the die and was moving my marker when a somber face followed the quiet knock. It was immediately apparent something was amiss.

"Aisha, I think it is best if you go home," she said gently. "Seun, Uncle wants you in his room."

"It was not me. It was already cracked," I was already protesting, sure Mrs. Folayo had found the mug I had broken and stashed at the back of the cupboard. Uncle rarely summoned me to his room and I was thinking of the best way to avoid a scolding. Uncle's red eyes and gentle voice surprised me when I walked into the room whose heavy curtains were mostly drawn.

"Seun," Uncle started quietly, his usually steady voice wavering slightly, "there was a military attack in Odi." The name of my hometown did not initially trigger anything in me and I continued to stare blankly at Uncle.

"Many people died," Uncle continued, his voice cracking completely and tears pooling in his eyes.

"Is mummy okay?" I cut in, in a panicked voice. Uncle's silence confirmed what his mouth could not.

"How about my sister and father?"

"Seun, everyone in your family . . . " Uncle was saying with unrestrained tears when I suddenly slumped to the ground.

Hassan Hajjaj,
Hindiii, 2011

JEAN-PIERRE BEKOLO and KENNETH HARROW

a conversation

Filmmakers at the frontlines

JEAN-PIERRE BEKOLO is a noted African film director from Cameroon. Bekolo's debut film *Quartier Mozart* (1992) won an award at the Cannes Film Festival and the film became the representative of a new generation that has been working against the restrictive expectations of African cinema, mixing genres and linking pop with politics. His publications such as *Africa for the Future Dagan* (2009) and video installations like "An African Woman in Space" at the Musée du Quai Branly Paris (2007–08) are intellectual and futuristic statements in their own right. His avant-garde political thriller *Les saignantes* (2005) was the first African sci-fi movie to be premiered at the Toronto Film Festival and was nominated in two categories at the French Césars in 2009. His new film, a 4-hour documentary *Les Choses et les mots de Mudimbe* is part of the official selection of the 2015 Berlinale.

Jean-Pierre Bekolo, one of Africa's most important artists, is an award-winning writer and director from Cameroon whose work addresses local and global audiences with its bold genre-blending and avant-garde aesthetics. His most recent film Le président *highlights the problem of Africa's cult-of-personality leaders who never seem to leave office. Bekolo engages in a spirited discussion with Kenneth Harrow, a leading authority on African cinema. Dictatorships, colonialism, African emancipation, the filmmaker's resistance and complicity, aesthetics and cinematic identification are only some of the topics they touch upon.*

Kenneth Harrow: Jean-Pierre, I was thinking about the films *Timbuktu* by Abderrahmane Sissako and your 2013 film *Le président*. They are films dealing with power and rule in Africa; and the transitions in and out of power. This very minute, we are watching the situation in Burkina Faso unfold

with troops of the army racing to the capital to contest the palace guards' attempted coup. The coup leader Gilber Diendere was a longtime associate of ousted president Blaise Compaoré, and his years in power were ended only by a popular uprising. Alongside the situation, one might consider the low-level fighting in Burundi where Nkurunziza (a two-term president) has now imposed his rule by forcing through a third term and the attempted military coup that failed to stop him. One thinks of Kagame forcing through legislative change permitting him a third term. One thinks of Assad, and Qaddhafi, or Bourghiba, rulers who wouldn't leave in a timely fashion, along with Biya seen in *Le président*, your film on that topic.

This isn't entirely a question, but I'm wondering, how are we to think of this, of Africa's rulers, its Mugabes, its Bongos, its Biyas, you name it, in power for so long? It seems too easy to say, make them democratic or that the West has solved this issue.

Jean-Pierre Bekolo: Ken, I have been thinking a lot about the very nature of cinema that we (I say, we African filmmakers) started producing in the early stage (the Sembène years . . .) and the cinema we are doing now, and all the steps it went through. At some point, perhaps because that cinema was born almost along with African nationalism and therefore independence, it took on the identity of being a tool, a medium, a means of emancipation of African people, a kind of utilitarian mission that later moved it to serve some of the purposes of NGOs. Some others pursued a kind of ethnological objective of explaining the complex African society to the western world. If I had to keep one thing that was key for me in the making of *Le président,* it was this idea of emancipation in a context marked by alienation. We can see this with

KENNETH HARROW is Distinguished Professor of English at Michigan State University. His work focuses on African cinema and literature, and Diaspora and Postcolonial Studies. He is the author of *Thresholds of Change in African Literature* (Heinemann, 1994), *Less Than One and Double: A Feminist Reading of African Women's Writing* (Heinemann, 2002), *Postcolonial African Cinema: From Political Engagement to Postmodernism* (Indiana UP, 2007), and *Trash! A Study of African Cinema from Below* (Indiana UP, 2013). He has edited numerous collections and written over 50 articles and a dozen chapters. He has organized numerous conferences dealing with African literature and cinema. He served as President of the African Literature Association, and was honored with their first Distinguished Member Award.

(Facing page) An African Woman in Space, 2007

the example of the role played by football which was supported by African regimes and yet was a means of alienation despite the fact that we all like it. The question is how do you pursue the initial cinema's emancipation project of the continent, in the Africa we live in today? Consider our behavior as film-makers who have emptied FESPACO (Panafrican Film and Television Festival of Ouagadougou) also of all its political meaning and substance, maybe since it was held in Burkina Faso, a country that symbolically assassinated that project of emancipation. And we as filmmakers accepted it.

We African filmmakers have partnered with our dictators for pragmatic reasons, I guess, and have now neutralized that project of emancipation of the continent. I can say that Congo's Balufu Bakupa-Kanyinda is with Kabila, Chad's Mahamat Saleh Haroun with Idriss Deby, Abderrahmane Sissako with Mohamed Ould Abdel Aziz, Bassek Ba Khobio with Paul Biya, Idrissa Oue-draogo, Gaston Kaboré, Fanta Nacro all with Blaise Compaore, etc. I remem-ber asking Balufu, why are you so happy now? You who were so angry at Compaoré (you see it in his film on Sankara), angry at neocolonialism, at the French, Belgium etc. Nothing has changed. Things might even be worse with the French military presence on the continent, the intervention in the killing of Qaddafi, their acts in taking out Laurent Gbagbo... but you, and everybody else, are content, what happened?

So we can't separate what we filmmakers have become from the films we are making in relation to these powers that are ruling Africa. Is it a deception in the relationship we expect to have with France as the financier of African cinema, the France that made us dream it was a democratic country that would accompany us in our emancipation project? It seems like we are mimicking the relationship France has with those dictators and therefore perpetuating them.

Kenneth Harrow: But what does it take to represent this in film? That's really the first question. I am thinking of the relationship between film, representation and political urgency. What are the constraints that are placed on cinema that keep it from falling into traps – commercial, political, ideological – that make it problematic to make a film about the need for a president to retire, an overdue retirement, or to make a film about a militant jihadist movement that takes over a town and destroys its culture. I wonder if it is impossible, even though you and Sissako have made your films on such topics.

Jean-Pierre Bekolo: In a letter I wrote to Abdoulaye Wade, then president of Senegal, that was published in *Jeune Afrique*, I appealed to Wade to support African cinema, which he sees as a transnational, panafrican African enterprise. I also told him that cinema is the frontline of engagement: "Dear President Wade, Africa is at war, a war of images, and we filmmakers are at the frontlines." The other thing that remains as unfinished in the same way as the emancipation project is the forms of our films themselves, so that one would have to say *Le président* is experimental, and it has to be. My feeling was that I had to play a three-part role: myself telling the story (as the filmmaker), as the subject (the President), as the audience (the Cameroonians). Whatever comes out of all this is an attempt to reconcile the three. And the theme is not chosen by coincidence: it's a topic that defines so much of our lives and our future on the continent; it gives the process another dimension and pushes us to redefine cinema for us and what its role could be in our existence today, even as a state/nation.

With *Le président* again, I was telling the Cameroonians about a man they

Scene from
Le Président, 2013

know better than me. So I had to find a form that doesn't really tell them the story of the president as much as gives them time while sitting in front of their screen to go with their mind where they are not otherwise allowed to go—maybe because of self-censorship, propaganda etc., facing the kind of meditation that they have been avoiding. This is where the typical narrative form could be alienating in some sense. Maybe here, the fact that my Cameroonian audience that is dealing with Paul Biya on a daily basis was my obsession, and this shaped the film the way it did. It was not like I was trying to tell to a global audience what's going on in Cameroon. I didn't want to mythologize the story as Sissako will do, or aestheticize it for no specific reason. There is no doubt that the audience in Cameroon got confused. This included the "censors," which also includes the French ambassador who said to me in a letter that *Le président* is political, and cannot be shown in the French Cultural Center because he has to be neutral in the fight between the two political entities (me and the regime). I believe that it is from such confusion and debates or controversies that we will be able to have an impact as filmmakers on our society, people, dictators, colonialists and so on.

Kenneth Harrow: Your letter to Wade and your response to my first set of questions gestures toward your own work, as well as that of others. There is no wiggle room that I see in the indictment of forces you see as nefarious in their roles in Africa. Bad leaders, authoritarianism, European (meaning French) attempts to continue to dominate "their" countries after independence has been won. Other threats come from the West's negative stereotyping of Africans which is particularly noxious for African youth who need positive self-images.

This protest is admirable and ennobling. You call it the project of emancipation, and lament that in all this time after independence it has not been realized; it animates your letter to Wade in which you beg the president to support African cinema so that we can see African images produced by African filmmakers to be shown to African audiences. A plea that really animated FEPACI (The Pan African Federation of Filmmakers or Fédération Panafricaine des Cinéastes) and the original activists who embraced Third Cinema, and sought to do something positive that would counter Hollywood, and its equivalent negative imaging in the films of other countries.

Yet at the same time, I resist your reactions despite sharing your embrace of the emancipation project. I don't think emancipation can be won by making films that exhort the audience, which is what positive self-images might be thought to accomplish. Just the opposite, I think the audience will be alienated when it senses that the filmmaker is telling them what to think. And maybe I don't even care if the audience takes it well or not; I think of emancipation in different terms.

I don't know how you can negotiate between the desire to educate an audience, to lecture to it, as if you have the truth and want to give it to them, and the desire to engage in a dialogue with the audience in which they are given their due respect as holders of their own opinions.

I am most intrigued by your notion that *Le président* is sustained by three poles. So now I can see you seeing yourself as an outsider presenting their president to them ("a man they know better than me"). Then you say you are giving them an opportunity, or permission, to think the unthinkable which was blocked "maybe because of self-consorship, propaganda, etc."—to critique their president, their éminence grise who is always there, behind the curtain, governing invisibly with a hand that somehow cannot be contested, despite the 1990s and his own losses. He would seem to embody something, like Mugabe or Bongo or Obiang Nguema, what Gabriel Garcia Márquez captures in *One Hundred Years of Solitude,* or what Sony Labou Tansi represented in the dictator-autocrat in his novel *Life and a Half* – the ridiculously inhuman embodiment of power that won't go away.

Jean-Pierre Bekolo: The term "emancipation" here is connected with the idea that Africans are not allowed to speak, that they (Europeans?) speak on their behalf in the same way Africans have no history. They could only exist through a European destiny, using European religion, European names, European knowledge . . . they even had to claim European ancestry—"nos ancêtres les gauls" (the gauls, our ancestors). That's the alienation that Ousmane Sembène's generation who experienced colonialism tried to overcome by taking a camera to emancipate themselves. If Sembène always signed his letter with "la lutte continue" (the struggle continues) it is because beyond the themes of his films, he considered that the "lutte" was not over. If I draw a parallel with Cameroon where the nationalists lost, we can consider it is still ruled with the DNA of the colonial alienation program, from Ahidjo to Biya.

Kenneth Harrow: The people of Cameroon can't see the real Biya; can't speak to him; can't influence him, despite his ubiquitous presence in their lives. You take on the role of the people in their need to address him, and when Vespero faces the camera and tells the implied president what the youth need, a scene which summarizes the entire project of the film, I see Bekolo addressing a Biya whom he cannot actually confront face to face. So you face him by writing to

Wade; by making this film and animating it with characters like a president whom you can address through the voices of characters throughout the film who respond to his words. And if it is inconceivable that in real life a real African president will really quit out of fatigue, or go underground and sneak out of his palace, or stop to chat with a popular rapper, well, film makes the inconceivable possible by offering a pact to the audience that it can share in the fantasy for an hour, and then safely go home without the police bothering them.

You address the Cameroonians as the audience, in your remarks above, telling them, here is your problem—you know it better than I, since I am only a pop voice you can enjoy, knowing your real lives and everyday struggles can't be overcome by a film about a mythic president who plays an aestheticized part. But maybe in the laughing, the nodding with the rapper, pointing up to the sky and telling you, young people, your day is coming—you will slyly seduce them to join in making this film. You can only do that if they join you in the fantasy of addressing not them, but Biya himself, the man on the billboard, and not the pretense of a president who regrets his past actions and failures, and who admits them to anyone who will listen, including in front of a camera.

So I refuse to take this direct address to the people as a tool of emancipation; I refuse to accept its summation of Biya's failures, no matter how accurate, and instead insist on hopping on one of those motos (seen frequently in the film) with three people on it already, continually manoeuvering through traffic not so as to force me to ask, where are we going, but rather so as to let the ride and the rider become a moment of liberation. It is very scary when two cars or a truck is coming toward you, and you turn around and look back at the camera in the car that is tracking your ride.

Most of all, bringing the people into a space where they normally don't go, aren't allowed to go, not because of Biya but because of their own adherence to notions of what a film is supposed to do, to the prisonhouse of the mind that has come to accept ideas of normalcy as right and proper—this is what I look for in the risky business of making real films for real people with real lives, and most of all, with real confidence in their ability to respond when called upon. That emancipation sets askew the question of selling out to the regimes in place, working within their aegis, as happened when Kabore's *Zan Boko* was made with the money of the very government and ministry he was critiquing.

For example, as it happened in your case, the French ambassador says, go ahead, make your political movies, they are great. But, he says, don't expect us to show them in our Cultural Centers because we are guests in Cameroon that will regulate its own cultural limits and political limits of tolerance. My question above all is, how is the regulation of the artist's relationship with power negotiated when a film is made and shown, and really what is the location where power and freedom meet in the struggle to dominate the other. Maybe Wade and Biya, two very old men who had known and still know one kind of power, are basically irrelevant to the project of emancipation which most of all still needs to be thought through. And I don't mean to say that the thinking through means we no longer share the dreams of emancipation of 55 years ago, but that we fail those dreams if we hold onto their notions of struggle in their days as being the keys to our freedom today.

Jean-Pierre Bekolo: A film like *Le président* is a profanation, a blasphemy to this thirty-three-years-in-power, godlike figure, but the film has no preachy intention. In my opinion the film is an intrusion into a sphere where cinema is not allowed, with its only intention being to disturb the established thirty-three-year-order of Cameroon. Now if the film is written, edited, and organized with the Cameroonian audience in mind, it is not because my intention was to dictate to the audience what they are supposed to think, but because like any author or filmmaker I am using the medium's language to play with the audience's fears, emotions, expectations etc. Here the montage as a language is used to produce a commentary on the situation in Cameroon where, for example, we see a long scene with prisoners planning to escape, but are never seen escaping. My intention was to raise the question of the powerful ministers who are in jail and who might be the alternative to Paul Biya when he is gone. Only Cameroonians might have those questions in their mind as the scene unfolds. It will bring Cameroonians onto that terrain of questioning the after-Biya. Its potential danger has produced an aesthetics, a form, a rhythm. What I do here is what cinema is supposed to do, unless cinema itself is now seen as an act of alienation as it tries to direct the audience in one direction or another. It is not as if one could watch a film that is not driven by a writer or a director's intention and which is trying to produce in the viewer a specific thought or emotion. (Did I get this right?) Whether he succeeds or not is another question.

I never said my films or any African film is an emancipation project. I oppose Sembène's view of cinema to counter colonialism as a whole, a colonialism whose project was the alienation of African identities, etc. The very idea for that early generation was that they could take a camera and film, and this was already an act of emancipation in the face of the colonialists. I think the French of that time had a term for people whom they could pick and who would be on the way to becoming the Africans they liked, one that was "civi-

lized": they were "les évolués." You can't apply that notion of emancipation as a preachy, lecturing cinema to the Cameroon audience.

Kenneth Harrow: What exactly is this emancipation about, and is alienation, as you are using it, its opposite? I gather from your initial statement about emancipation that it is a mental decolonization. But the target shifts from the French, in Sembène's day, to Biya today. For me the mental goals of decolonization from the metropole can't be the same as those of freeing oneself from the *main mise* of a strongman autocrat, or however you might want to call Biya. The issues of African identity, language, history, culture, selfhood— all pretty complicated notions that begin to come apart when examined closely—are different from complicity with an authoritarian regime. What alienation does Biya impose upon Cameroonians, other than their submission to his government as more or less inevitable. I've heard more than a few Cameroonians say, he isn't great but he's better than the others—whoever they might be. There seems to be a total disillusionment with the political process providing anything we could imagine as rallying the population, as happened in the 1990s. It is curious how the colonial project completely vanishes in your reading of Paul Biya. Why is that the case?

Jean-Pierre Bekolo: Paul Biya is a French colonial product, he is running Cameroon with many French colonial principles, including repression, where we can see some of the methods of *la guerre psychologique anti-révolutionnaire* developed by the French during the Indochina war. He still runs the country with a team of people who from 1960 on, after independence, took over the French dirty job of repressing the nationalist UPC movement. Indeed these

(Facing page) An African Woman in Space, 2007

movements have lost, and 1990 was the second time they also lost: the disillusionment is something losers develop I guess.

Kenneth Harrow: Is countering colonialism the same as countering autocracy? More important to me, are the aesthetics that you identify as being produced in the struggle against Biya different from those of Sembène and his generation? The difference I see is profound. Sembène worked on an ideological level that was commensurate with realism, or with realisms, be they historical, social, or political. He wanted the audience to identify with the characters, as in *Mandabi*, and with their plight. In all his films these qualities were there: plight and identification, so as to educate and then mobilize.

Jean-Pierre Bekolo: The story of identification in cinema in Africa is very interesting. Do you think African audiences would have been able to watch Chinese Kung Fu films, Indian melodrama musicals, American Hollywood films if there were no identification? We can't deny that identification comes into play when a child's attention is lured by another child in a film or that the main reason of the success of Nollywood derives from Africans seeing Africans—for the first time people seeing other people that look like them, filling their screens. If cinema can't go beyond the reality African youth are trapped in and that could still make interesting cinema, it doesn't mean that that audience has no ability to project itself into another reality where a young woman could replace Paul Biya. Isn't it also the function of cinema to break that screen of the real? Even if people in Cameroon, immersed in their reality, do not envision Paul Biya leaving, Paul Biya will leave. They have no idea of how it is going to happen, and the fact that they might not identify with any actor of that scenario doesn't mean cinema can't allow them to do so. Cinema is asking the "what if" question; *Le président* is speculating about an inevitable future Cameroonians are reluctant to address.

Kenneth Harrow: How has it been to have experienced life abroad and at home, on and off, in creating *Le président* or *Les saignantes*, which contain ostensibly very powerful criticisms of your home country, while also being at home in Europe, and in European or American techniques/technology of a cinematic vision, with a practice and a sensibility that is marked so strongly by hyper-modernist split-screen hip hop youth culture elements. Your essay "What is cinema" also leads to the question, what is the filmmaker in all this, and finally—as I love to ask what I am not supposed to ask—who do you think you are? How much do you feel having lived in France for so long shaped your way of thinking about making movies? How much does it shape your way of thinking about the politics of France, in the world, and in Africa?

Jean-Pierre Bekolo: It is funny how we Cameroonians like to compare the Germans and the French even though we were colonized by both. And I asked Professor David Simo, a German studies professor at the University of Yaounde that question: "Who between the French and the Germans are the most racist?" He gave me an answer he had heard from an older person who happened to live under both: "Tu me demandes de choisir entre la peste et le choléra?" (You are asking me to choose between the plague or cholera?)

To answer your question about identity and the different cultures I have encountered and the idea of assimilation, I always like to use the case of Cameroonian sax player Manu Dibango who left Cameroon at the age of fourteen in 1947. He hasn't lost even his Cameroonian accent. His music for sure has a lot of western, African American and Congolese influence. Another interesting figure also from Cameroon and also in music is Francis Bebey. I think his African culture came more from studying Pygmies as an ethnologist than from his cultural immersion as a Douala. I learnt more about the Beti culture by becoming friends with Philippe Laburthe Tolra (as we tried to adapt his book *Le Tombeau du Soleil* into a film). I read about the ritual of Mevungu (used in *Les saignantes*) in his book. I had my first Ewondo email experience with Professor Lluis Mallart, a Spanish ethnologist who studied Beti as he wrote to me in Ewondo. . . .

Who are we once we start moving, absorbing other cultures and influences? Is it about becoming? The process of becoming has many paths I guess. But becoming what? That is your question. Being an individual, something unique emerges, calibrated by your origins, and the encounters—the people you meet and your profession. In my case I think cinema is what I use in everything: I think, I write, I engage with Cameroon politics as a filmmaker. What I see when I land from the airplane, I see people who are not myself. And I really see people are the same wherever I go. The most difficult part is to convince people who are in the same spot that they are like the others I met 6000 kilometers away. This is what I argue in the "An African Woman in Space," an installation I did at the Quai Branly on Diaspora. It doesn't matter where you go, we are run by the "indigenous" who use the fact that their parents, grand-parents, great-grand-parents were from that spot to make decisions for those who move around and who accumulate a lot by moving.